I0551743

# DESTINY

## A Story of Mary Queen of Scots
### and her lady-in-waiting
### Mary Seton

## Anne Kinsey

# DESTINY

## A Story of Mary Queen of Scots

### And her lady-in-waiting, Mary Seton

Copyright © 2011 Anne Kinsey

All rights reserved.

ISBN-13: 978-0615574028

Castell Books

# PRELUDE
# FOTHERINGAY CASTLE,
# ENGLAND, 1587

Thirteen-year-old Clare Paulet pushed aside the brocaded, pine-green bed curtains. She listened for a moment, and when she didn't hear anything except the wind at the shutters, she reached for her slippers and robe. Once dressed, she lifted the night candle from the table beside her bed, and protecting the flame with her cupped hand, crept into the corridor.

It was one of those February nights when you know spring is coming. The chill was gone from the air and the corridor was less drafty, but the gray stone walls were cold to the touch with beads of moisture gathered in the crevices. The corridor was lit by torches set in metal holders along the wall. The floor rushes, rustling and crunching as she stepped over them, were mixed with rosemary and jasmine and gave off a spicy scent. The queen of Scotland, who was imprisoned in this castle, wanted the floor rushes to be clean and sweet smelling at all times. Even though she was a prisoner here, she was still treated like a queen and all such wishes were obeyed.

Once in the west wing, Clare paused on the threshold of Lady Mary Seton's room. The door was opened wide enough for Clare to peek in. Lady Mary sat facing a window in a hard-backed chair under the light of a single wax candle. She sat so straight that her back didn't touch the chair at all. The candlelight, reflected in the window, showed the lines of her face.

"Lady Mary," Clare whispered.

She didn't move. Then, a bit louder, Clare repeated, "Lady Mary?"

Mary Seton gave a slight jolt as if awakened from sleep and put her hand to her throat. "You frightened me to death, child," she said.

"I'm sorry."

"It's all right. We are all a little jumpy tonight. You may come in."

Mary Seton's room was as austere as she was. The only decor was a single crucifix mounted over the bed and an assortment of ivory and pewter statues of the Virgin Mary near the corner where she knelt to pray each morning.

"Is there any news?" Lady Mary asked.

"My father said that Queen Elizabeth still won't sign the death warrant."

Mary Seton gave her head the slightest shake to show her amazement. "Maybe she won't sign it after all. The queen of England does what she pleases. She is as capricious as the wind." Lady Mary's lips were a thin line, her pale, watery blue eyes hard and cold. "It's late," she said. "You should be in bed."

"I wanted to bring you the news. I knew it would make you happy." Because Lady Mary spent her days with the queen of Scots and the queen's other attendants, late at night was the only time Clare could catch her alone. She still couldn't get over her amazement that the queen of Scots was here, in their castle. The queen, of course, had no time for Clare. Like everyone else, she suspected the end was near, so she spent her days writing letters. But sometimes, if Clare caught Lady Mary Seton all alone and in the right mood, she would sit with Clare and talk to her.

Now was evidently one of those times. "You may stay for a few minutes, if you like." Lady Mary pointed to a nearby stool.

Clare sat down eagerly.

"I suppose you want more stories," said Lady Mary

"Oh, I do! Thank you!"

Something almost like a smile came to Lady Mary's face. "I suppose I need the diversion. Perhaps you'd like to hear about the queen's wedding in Paris."

"I would! It must have been magnificent!"

"It was indeed."

"Please tell me about it!"

"The queen of Scots rode in a litter draped with white satin. She wore all white except a gold crown set with rubies and sapphires. A Swiss guard led the wedding parade. Musicians dressed in yellow and red played trumpets and drums. Thousands of people lined the streets of Paris, just to catch a glimpse of her."

Lady Mary's voice was detached and she talked as if she were reciting a memorized speech, or performing a duty. She spoke as if the memories didn't thrill her. Perhaps the wedding itself hadn't thrilled her. Lady Mary was so reserved, it was hard to imagine her being thrilled by anything.

To keep Mary Seton talking, Clare said, "The queen must have been so happy on her wedding day."

"She was. I believe that was the happiest day of her life."

It occurred to Clare that Lady Mary always talked about the times when the queen was happy or afraid or in trouble. She never talked about herself. "Were you happy then, too?" Clare asked.

"Me?" Lady Mary blinked, as if startled by the question.

"When were you happiest?"

Mary Seton sat quietly, not moving at all. Clare thought she was remembering something she would share, but then she said, "My life has been one of duty. I have served my queen, and this has been my sole happiness."

It was a correct, obligatory answer, but her voice sounded too tight and Clare suspected there were things she wasn't telling. From Mary Seton's stories, Clare already knew so much about the Scottish queen and her exciting life, beginning with how she became queen of Scotland when she was an infant, only a week old and her father died after facing the English in battle. But all Clare knew about Lady Mary was that she had been one of the famous four Marys, four little girls, all named Mary like the queen, who had been chosen to be her childhood playmates.

Lady Mary fingered the locket she wore at her waist. Clare knew she was overstepping and asking a question which was too personal, but she couldn't resist: "Whose picture do you wear?"

"My queen's, of course. I wore this same locket, with a different picture of her, at her wedding in Paris."

She snapped open the locket to show a miniature of the Scottish queen. The picture, so different from the matronly white-haired queen imprisoned in Fotheringhay Castle, showed a young girl with a pretty oval-shaped face, sweetly curved bow-shaped lips, and amber eyes matching her golden red hair.

"Is it a good likeness?" Clare asked. "Did she have such a sweet face?"

"No painting ever completely captured her beauty. You can see she was pretty, with lovely coloring, but her real beauty was in the light that shone in her eyes like a candle."

The facing picture in the locket was of a man. Unlike the queen's other ladies-in-waiting, Mary Seton had never married. She had taken a vow of chastity and planned to enter a nunnery when the queen no longer needed her company. Clare assumed, therefore, that the man was a brother or nephew.

"And the other picture?" Clare asked.

Lady Mary looked into the locket. "His name was Alexander Beaton." Before Clare could get a good look at the picture, Lady Mary closed the locket.

"Alexander Beaton?" said Clare. "Wasn't one of the four Marys named Mary Beaton?"

"Yes," said Mary Seton quietly. "Alexander was her cousin."

Clare wondered if it could be that this pious lady had once had a lover. It occurred to her that if Mary Queen of Scots were a figure of romance, Lady Mary Seton was a mystery, an enigma.

Clare simply could not imagine the staid Mary Seton as a girl of fifteen at the queen's wedding. Had she giggled and whispered secrets, like other girls? Or, as lady-in-waiting to a child queen, had she, even then, been reserved and quiet?

# PART I
# MARY SETON

Are you not weary in your distant places,
Far, far from Scotland of the mists and storm;
In drowsy airs the sun smite on your face,
The days so long and warm?
When all around you lie strange hearts sleeping;
Those lands where no fond memories lie,
Do not your sad hearts over seas come leaping,
To the Highlands and the Lowlands of your home?
*-Scottish folk song*

# PARIS, 1558

# CHAPTER 1

Mary Seton picked up her skirts and ran to the arched trellis leading to the formal palace gardens. She had pleaded a headache that morning to escape her duties. For the past week, in preparation for the queen's wedding, she'd had to endure hour after hour of tiresome audiences and ceremonies. But this morning, with the sun shining and the sky a bright, cloudless blue, she couldn't bear standing in her decorative place in the presence chamber any longer.

She breathed a sigh of relief when she reached the orchards at the far end of the gardens. She had escaped. Nobody would find her here, in the thickets near the brook. The apple trees were in blossom, sweetening the air with their fragrance. In a grassy spot near the brook in the shade of a cluster of oaks, she took off her slippers and stockings and splashed her feet in the water.

She pulled off her heart-shaped cap and shook her head, freeing her hair. Her hair was the exact color of the sandy pebbles at the bottom of the brook. When she relaxed, as she was now, there was a sweet timidity about her face, but around other people she always held herself stiffly, her face tense, her expression austere.

Laughter rang out behind her. Startled, she scooped up her shoes and stockings and ducked behind a hedge. The laugh came again and she recognized Mary Fleming, another of the queen's four Marys. She heard a man's voice and even before catching a glimpse of his face, she knew that Mary Fleming's companion was Henri, the Prince of Conde's son.

Mary Fleming, the boldest of the queen's four Marys, with bright blue eyes and shiny black hair, was proud of her close kinship to the Scottish queen. Although the line was illegitimate, she was the queen's cousin, and was thus given precedence among the queen's ladies.

Laughing, holding onto Henri's arm, Mary Fleming moved into the sunshine of a small clearing, less then twenty feet from Mary Seton.

"You know I shouldn't be here." Mary Fleming lifted her fan as if to hide a blush.

Henri caught her arms. "I had to see you again."

Mary Fleming said, "My queen would think me disloyal if she knew I was here. How can I be disloyal to my queen?"

"What of your loyalty to me? You know I have loved you, longed for you—"

Their talk irritated Mary Seton, who had no wish to witness the kind of scene she had seen many times before. Mary Fleming cared nothing for Henri. Flirting, her favorite pastime, was made all the more exciting for her because Henri was a Protestant and an enemy. Mary Seton ducked away so Mary Fleming and Henri wouldn't see her when they emerged from behind the hedge. She glanced back once to see Mary Fleming put her arms around Henri's neck.

Mary Seton sighed. There was simply no place she could go to escape and be alone. The life of a courtier was a public life, and Mary Seton found it tiring to be on her guard all the time. She needed time alone, when she could relax and look inward and bring order and calm to her inner world.

Once she was far enough away from Mary Fleming and Henri so that they wouldn't find her, she sat on a smoothly polished marble bench facing a bed of white lilies.

But then a group of ladies emerged from the path. When they came close enough, Mary recognized them as attendants of Catherine de Medici, queen of France, who was soon to be Mary Queen of Scots' mother-in-law. They were gossiping about the Scots noblemen who had recently arrived for the wedding, laughing about how rustic and ridiculous they were. They seemed not to know, or care, that Mary Seton was close enough to hear them talking, and that her own brother was among the Scots noblemen who had journeyed to France for the wedding. Or perhaps they knew she was nearby, and they wanted her to hear.

Such insults didn't bother Mary Seton at all. She didn't care what people said. What she didn't like was being forced to give up her hope for a few moments of peace and privacy. After one last wistful look at the beds of graceful white irises, she reluctantly returned to her duties in the Scottish queen's presence chamber.

That night was the first of the queen's wedding celebrations. Mary Seton stood in the brightly lit ballroom surrounded by ladies whispering behind their fans. Glass chandeliers with thousands of candles lit the ballroom. The Scottish queen's Guise relatives had ordered the decorations. Bouquets of roses and lilies were displayed in gilded vases and the balconies were hung with silken banners. Glittering high on the wall, the royal Scottish coat of arms was linked with the Guise emblem.

Mary Seton stood alone, as stiff as the marble pillar behind her, uncomfortable in her gown which was laced too tightly. She wore a midnight-blue velvet gown with an embroidered stomacher. The neck was square-cut and the long sleeves hung almost to the floor. She wore no jewelry except a small silver cross at her throat. Her waist was pinched because Mary

Fleming had insisted on pulling her stays until she thought she'd faint. "You're pretty enough," Mary Fleming had said, "but your lacing should be tighter. And you need more rouge or people will think you are not interested in dancing."

"Maybe she isn't interested in dancing," said Mary Beaton, another of the four Marys. "Maybe she really likes sitting alone for hours. Maybe sitting in the gardens reading poetry really is more fun than dancing."

Mary Fleming was called the 'flower of the Marys,' and with her vibrant coloring, she was indeed striking. But Mary Beaton, with her pale blonde hair and soft gray eyes, had her share of admirers as well. Mary Beaton could usually be found trailing behind Mary Fleming, as if drawing energy from her.

"Maybe she's still dreaming of falling in love," Mary Fleming said.

"No, no," said Mary Beaton. "She prefers the convent and wants to be a nun."

Once, in a moment of indiscretion, Mary Seton made the mistake of telling Mary Fleming that she planned to marry for love. Mary Fleming had laughed at the absurdity of it. "Only peasant girls marry for love," she had said. She'd been teasing Mary Seton about it ever since.

Mary Livingston, Mary Seton's closest friend at court, came to her rescue. "Leave her alone," she told the others. "Just because she doesn't like trouble, the way you do, only means she has more sense."

Now, in the brightly lit ballroom, Mary Seton watched as a gentleman of the king's chamber approached Mary Fleming, and bowed to her from the waist. She accepted him with a curtsy, and they moved to the line of dancers forming at the center of the ballroom floor. The music picked up in tempo, and the gentlemen handed their swords to the nearest pages. Several of the Scotsmen who had come to France for the wedding now joined the dancers. Although not trained in court etiquette by the rigors of a French education, these Scottish noblemen knew well enough the meaning of courtly flattery.

"Mary Fleming," one said, "you are most bewitching."

"The flower of the queen's Marys," said another.

Mary Seton stood alone, watching the dancers. Then she saw a Scotsmen approach Mary Beaton, and talk familiarly with her. Most of the Scotsmen who had come to the wedding – including Mary Seton's brother – wore French clothing. This man, though, wore animal-skin boots laced to the knees and a traditional Scottish fur mantle. He seemed completely out of place amid the elaborate décor, and not just because of his clothing. There was something in his expression which marked him as one who observed closely. His eyes were soft brown, his features gentle, but there was a strength in the set of his jaw and intelligence in his eyes.

Mary Seton jumped to a tap on her arm.

Mary Livingston laughed. "Sorry to startle you. What were you thinking about?"

Mary Seton managed to shake her head, as if at nothing. She wanted to meet the man who was standing with Mary Beaton, but she had long ago formed the habit of hiding her intimate thoughts even from her closest friends.

"I have to keep an eye on you. Maybe Mary Fleming is right. If not for us, you would fade into the walls." Mary Livingston took her arm and led her into the thickest part of the crowd. "You have absolutely no business standing alone."

A group of courtiers and wedding guests moved to admit them.

Mary Seton looked up to see a thin man about thirty with a long face and strong features watching her. A moment passed before she realized that he was an Englishman, Christopher Norton, the eldest son of Earl Norton. This was the man her family wanted her to marry. Mary's stomach lurched at the sight of him and she wished she could slip away and vanish. She looked around, but there was no hope of escape.

Norton smiled at her. There was nothing wrong with the way he smiled, and some might even think him handsome, but something about him, which Mary Seton could not define, repulsed her.

He walked toward her. "I thought I recognized you," he said. "Surely you remember me?"

"Of course," she said stiffly.

Mary Fleming joined them. She couldn't have known about the marriage negotiations, but she did know Norton's rank. Mary Fleming watched as Norton reached for Mary Seton's hand.

"You are even lovelier than I remembered, Lady Mary," he said.

Mary Seton nodded to acknowledge the compliment and then withdrew her hand.

When Norton turned away to talk to another gentleman who joined them, Mary Fleming touched Mary Seton's elbow and whispered, "Don't you know who he is?"

"Don't you remember what happened the last time he was here?" After paying extravagant compliments to Mary Seton, none of which she had believed, he had been discovered the next morning on the banks beyond the orchards, in the arms of a serving girl.

"He was indiscreet, that's all," Mary Fleming whispered.

Christopher Norton turned back to Mary Seton and said, "May I have the next dance?"

"Thank you, but I would really rather—"

"She would love to dance," Mary Fleming said, pushing them toward the dance floor.

Trapped, Mary Seton let him take her hand. He wore a purple cloak trimmed with gold and a long feather in the brim of his cap. He held her tightly and a large purple sapphire ring pressed into her hand. She stiffened until he loosened his grip.

Again she caught sight of Mary Beaton and the dark-haired man. What was it about him, she wondered, which so appealed to her? Perhaps it was the attentiveness in his bearing and the alertness of his expression, as if he was acutely aware of everything happening in the room. His attitude, however, wasn't fawning and awed, like so many of the guests.

"Lady Mary, you dance beautifully," Norton said. If he noticed her watching another man, he gave no indication.

"You speak like a Frenchman," she said smoothly, "so full of compliments and flattery."

His smiled deepened. He evidently took her words as a compliment when she hadn't meant them that way at all. She smiled, too. What a fool he was.

When they were at the closest place in the line to Mary Beaton and the gentleman, Mary Seton said, "I'm quite out of breath. We must stop for a few minutes."

Her ploy worked. Mary Beaton, seeing her, said to her companion, "Come, Alexander. I want you to meet Mary Seton."

Mary Beaton introduced Alexander Beaton, and she introduced Christopher Norton. Mary Beaton, evidently recognizing Norton's name, smiled coyly at him.

The music faded into silence. Everyone turned as the Duke of Guise, the Scottish queen's uncle, snapped his fingers in command. Twelve artificial sailboats trimmed in gold were wheeled onto the ballroom floor, their silver sails appearing to blow in a breeze.

"The boats," the duke announced, "symbolize a happy journey through life." At the helm of each boat was a member of the French royal family who chose as his partner the lady of his dreams.

The queen of Scots rode the first boat with the dauphin. She wore all white, her favorite color because it set off her warm, glowing coloring to perfection. Her cheeks were tinged with apricot, her hair, which had been red when she'd been younger, was now a rich auburn. She was positively glowing. In fact, Mary Seton knew from her deep flush that she was almost incoherent with happiness. Looking at her now, Mary Seton felt a smile come to her own face. It was impossible to see her joy and not share some of it.

The dauphin, in comparison, was pallid and thin, and

stood almost a full a head shorter than his bride. The pale fourteen-year-old seemed to draw a breath of life from his exuberant childhood companion who had now become his wife. Unkind gossips said the dauphin was too sickly and weak to father a child, and indeed, he seemed not to have reached puberty yet.

The Duke of Guise stepped forward and clapped his hands for attention. The entire room fell silent.

"We have joined the Scottish and French coat of arms," he said, "to symbolize the alliance of Scotland and France, which through this marriage, shall endure forever."

There was enthusiastic applause.

Alexander shook his head and whispered. "Does he think we don't know the truth? Scotland is on the verge of rebellion!"

"Alexander, hush," Mary Beaton hissed. "Someone may hear you."

"Did I forget the rules again?" He made a mock bow to Mary Seton. "Forgive me if I forget my manners and accidentally speak the truth. I am not accustomed to court life. This is my first time here."

"And it may be your last, if you don't act properly," said Mary Beaton. When he tried to loosen the ruff at his neck, Mary Beaton pushed his hand down. "And stop fidgeting. Honestly, Alexander. You are behaving like a peasant."

"Peasants do have certain advantages." He turned to Mary Seton and said, "Do you have to dress like this all the time?"

A giggle rose in Mary Seton's throat, but she stifled it. Her stays were much too tight. If she laughed, they would burst. Now that she looked closely into his face, she could see that he was young, probably not more than seventeen or eighteen. He spoke French perfectly, but with the Scottish accent that Mary Seton and the others had lost.

"Alexander," Mary Beaton said sternly. "We went to a lot of trouble to get you invited. Do not embarrass us, please."

"Let me explain," Alexander said to Mary Seton. "I am

nothing but the younger son of an untitled branch of the Beaton family. So I am supposed to be grateful for the honor of being allowed into the palace. I just hope I don't get locked in."

"Don't pay any attention to him," Mary Beaton advised Mary Seton. "He likes to hear himself talk." She turned away to smile at Christopher Norton.

Mary Seton became uncomfortably aware that Alexander was studying her. "You do look as proud as they say," he whispered. "You could be taken for a princess, but not a French princess. You're too restrained to be a French anything. I think you're supposed to simper more. See how my cousin does it?"

Mary Beaton was, just then, simpering at Christopher Norton.

"If you start mocking me," Mary Seton said, "I will see that you *are* locked in. A few weeks here should tame your wild tongue."

She smiled, enjoying his surprise.

Christopher Norton turned back to her. "Lady Mary, shall we dance again?"

The thought of dancing with Norton again repulsed her, but she couldn't think of how to refuse. They were all watching her. Embarrassed, she opened her fan. She knew she was flushing. "I couldn't really," she said. "Maybe Mary Beaton wants to dance."

Obligingly, Norton turned to Mary Beaton. Mary Seton watched, relieved, as they went to join the dancers.

"Well, done," Alexander said. "So you can simper when you want to."

That was it. She'd had enough of the entire ball, including his mockery. She wanted to get far away and hide.

But just then, in a much gentler voice, Alexander, watching Norton, said, "Who is he?"

"Nobody," said Mary Seton. Nobody except possibly her future husband. "He's the eldest son of Lord Norton."

"And you didn't want to dance with him?"

"Not for a minute."

When he smiled, all the gentleness came back into his face, and it was hard to believe he had just spent the past ten minutes making fun of everything to do with the court ball, including her.

"I must admit," he said, "that I have heard plenty about the grand Lady Mary Seton. I didn't expect her to be anything like you."

"What have you heard?"

"That you are the proudest and most aloof of the queen's Marys, the sister of the great Lord Seton, seventh Premier Baron of Scotland." He made a mock bow.

"They say all that?"

"More. They say you are the most pious and untouchable of the Marys. Even the French respect your family name, but you prefer convent life. They say you secretly want to be a nun."

"That just shows what *they* know."

He was standing so near and looking at her so closely that for a moment she thought he would take her hands and lead her to the dance floor. But abruptly the music ended. Mary Beaton and Norton were walking toward them. She watched gratefully as Mary Beaton took Norton's arm, momentarily distracting him. Instantly she stepped behind a group of ladies. Alexander followed her.

"He is going to come looking for me," she said. "I know it."

"Who? The nobody who is also the eldest son of an earl?"

"Out here," she said, ducking past a tapestry that hung over the entrance to a corridor. "This leads to the gardens."

"Is this happening?" he said. "Am I being taken into a darkened corridor by a future nun?"

"I am not a future nun. And it's not dark at the other end."

A large arched window with a waist-high railing looked out over the gardens, which were flooded now with torch light.

Pairs of ladies and gentlemen, their colorful satins and silks shimmering in the light, wandered about the rows of flowers and trees.

Mary leaned against the railing with Alexander beside her.

There is a certain beauty here," he said.

"Oh, yes," she agreed. "It's dazzling. But it's all surface, all glitter."

"You are not happy here," he said.

"No, I never have been."

He looked at her with a mixture of astonishment and respect. "Nobody knows that."

In moments like these, when he wasn't mocking her, she liked what she saw in his face: a quiet wisdom, a good-natured understanding of all he saw, and the boldness to call it what it was. Of course, there were plenty of people who visited the court – and some who lived here – who were outspoken and bold and critical of the Guises and their politics, but Alexander sparkled with humor and irony, not the cynicism she was used to.

"My cousin would not trade this life for anything in the world," he said. "She told me that you want to be a nun."

"Everyone thinks that because I prefer the Convent of Saint Pierre to the court." Just saying the name, Convent of Saint Pierre, was enough to conjure up an image of the perfect peace that was there, the beautiful gardens overgrown with wildflowers.

"That isn't what you really want?" he asked.

She felt entirely startled by the question. It occurred to her that nobody ever asked her what she really wanted. People either told her what she would do, or made assumptions about what she wanted.

"No," she said quietly. "That's not what I want."

"What do you want?"

She knew the answer to that question, but how could she tell this man, a perfect stranger, her desires – that she longed to fall in love with a man who would rescue her from court life?

"Tell me," he urged.

What she said was, "I want to live a simple, private life."

Alexander touched the locket at her waist and asked, "Whose picture do you wear?" She opened the locket to show a miniature portrait of the Scottish queen.

"It's a beautiful picture," he said.

"She is beautiful. Everything about her is beautiful. She is kind and good."

He looked at her closely as if to gage the truth of her words. But Mary Seton, unlike most courtiers, never flattered insincerely. "You may make fun of anything about the French court," she said, "but you may not mock her."

"May I speak the truth?" said Alexander. "Her uncles are doing her a great disservice. There are troubles in Scotland now, serious troubles. She is queen of Scotland, but she leaves the ruling to her French uncles, and the Scots despise the rule of French foreigners."

Like the queen, Mary Seton knew very little of the turmoil in Scotland. She'd often been told that the French armies and the queen's powerful Guise uncles could manage the unruly Scots. She'd also been told by many people, including her own brother, a Scottish baron, that most of the Scots were grateful to have the French as protectors. She'd been told this so often she believed it.

"I feel very certain—"

Just then someone called her name. Startled, she turned as Viola, who had been her governess and was now her lady's maid, strode toward them. "There you are, my dear. Your brother is looking for you."

"Please excuse me," Mary said to Alexander. She followed Viola back into the ballroom. It was impossible to escape, even for a minute, the eyes that watched her constantly.

George, the Seventh Premier Baron of Scotland, and the oldest of her half-brothers, was waiting for her just inside, standing next to Christopher Norton.

There were those who said she and George bore a family resemblance. They had the same thin features and gray eyes, but in his face was a sharp shrewdness. In hers was gentleness and sweetness.

"Mary, there you are," George said. "You remember Christopher Norton, I hope?"

"Of course," she said.

"We had the pleasure of dancing," Norton said, "not long ago." He extended his hand to Mary and said, "I hope you will dance with me again. They're starting a galliard."

"Oh, I don't think so—" The galliard was a lively, complex dance and she didn't think she could manage it just then.

"Go on, Mary," George urged.

Again, feeling trapped, she let Norton lead her to the dancers. "Really, my Lady Mary, you are most lovely," he said.

This time the compliment deeply irritated her. She wasn't lovely – not the way Mary Beaton or the queen was lovely – and she could tell from the way he dutifully spoke the words that he didn't mean it. He was holding her hand tightly, and pulled her too close to him. In the crowd, she caught a glimpse of Alexander Beaton watching them.

"You don't need to flatter me now," she said. "My brother cannot hear us."

"But he can see us," he said gripping her hand more tightly. "So please smile."

Oh! How dare he? She flushed with anger. Then the room spun and she thought she would faint. She pulled away from him so abruptly he had to let go. She put her fingers to her temples and squeezed her eyes closed. Strands of hair had escaped from her cap and clung damply to the sides of her face.

In the next moment, George was standing beside her. "Mary? Are you all right? You look ill!"

That was the excuse she needed. "I do not feel at all well," she said. "Perhaps if I lie down, I will feel better tomorrow."

"Yes, of course."

The night candles were already burning in the room she shared with the other Marys, and the bed curtains were pulled back. To get rid of Viola, Mary sent her to the apothecary for a medicine to soothe her stomach.

There were two curtained beds in the room, each large enough to sleep six or seven people comfortably, but luxuriously the four Marys slept two to a bed. Closing the curtains created a space as dark as night and as large as a room. Opposite her bed was a window seat with cushions of embroidered silk overlooking the inner courtyards. During the day she liked to sit here watching the activity in the courtyard. From sunup to vespers, horses clicked across the cobblestones, cartwheels squeaked, dozens of tradesmen in long coarse woolen cloaks, ribbon-sellers, perfumers, dressmakers, and apothecaries, came to sell their wares to the ladies and gentlemen of the court.

The courtyards were now quiet. She blew out her candle and pressed her cheek to the window's cool iron tracery that barred the room like a prison.

She had told Alexander she wanted a simple, private life.

Her own life thus far had been anything but private. Indeed, her life, from her earliest childhood, had been closely linked to the Scottish queen. In fact, from the time she was five and had left the nursery of Seton Castle to join the queen, her own family had been strangers to her, known to her only through letters and messages. The love she should have felt for her own family, she felt instead for the Scottish queen.

When King James IV of Scotland died leaving his infant daughter queen of Scotland, the most important political question facing the kingdom was who the young queen would one day marry, for whoever she married would become king of Scotland.

England and France had been fighting for generations over control of Scotland, which served as a convenient backdoor to

England. It was clear to both the king of France and the king of England that the easiest way to get hold of Scotland was to marry the little queen to one or the other of their sons.

When the little queen was four years old, the English armies, headed by that notorious bully King Henry the Eighth invaded Scotland for the purpose of kidnapping the child queen. He wanted to bring her to England, raise her in his own court, and when she grew up, marry her to his son, Edward.

But the queen's mother, a daughter of the house of Guise, had no desire for her daughter to be kidnapped by the English and raised as the future queen of England, so in the middle of the night, the little queen was spirited away and hidden on the secluded Isle of Inchamahome. Meanwhile, the queen's mother, through emissaries to France and with the help of a few Scottish lords who, at the time, were agreeable to any plan that would save them from the English, brought about the marriage treaty between the queen of Scots and the dauphin. As soon as the treaty was signed, she made the arrangements to send the queen of Scots to France for safety, to be raised at the French court and prepared for her future role as queen of France.

It was then that four little girls were chosen from the noble houses of Scotland to accompany her to France. Mary Seton's father and grandmother worked hard to get Mary Seton included in the little queen's retinue. Mary Seton was selected because of the Seton family's history of loyalty to the Scottish crown. Over the centuries of constant warfare and plots of treason, no Seton had ever once betrayed the crown. No other clan could make such a boast.

Mary Seton met the queen and the other three Marys one gray and misty morning. She rode on horseback with her father to Dumbarton Castle, a sandstone castle topped with battlements on a slight imminence, where the queen awaited the French flagships that would take her to France.

The windows of Dumbarton Castle, like the windows in

the Seton Castle, were small and high – little more than slits in the walls, for these castles had been built as military fortresses and not luxury palaces. Candles set in crystal chandeliers hung from the ceilings.

When Mary was led into the nursery, she felt shy, unsure what to say to a little girl her own age who was also her queen. In the room, a lady wearing velvet robes sat on a straight-backed chair with a piece of needlework in her lap. Four little girls were kneeling on a quilted comforter with several dolls arranged around them.

"I present Lady Mary Seton," the attendant said.

Instantly all four girls looked up. Mary Seton knew instantly which was the queen because the girl with the red hair and light sprinkling of freckles jumped to her feet and said, "Mary Seton! We've been waiting for you!"

The little queen gave her a hug.

Mary Seton loved her instantly. The girls moved to make room for her on the comforter. She sat with her feet tucked under her. Nervously, she arranged the folds of her skirts and petticoats around her.

She looked down at the dolls and drew in her breath, immediately forgetting her nervousness. The dolls were the most beautiful she had ever seen. One doll wore an aqua blue satin dress trimmed with white ribbon, the face exquisitely painted on porcelain with a tiny upturned mouth and carefully drawn eyelashes. Not a detail was overlooked, from the lacing of the bodice to the blue ribbons braided through the hair.

Forgetting her anxiety and shyness, Mary Seton said, "Oh! She's beautiful!"

She reached for the doll and turned it over in her hands.

In the next instant, she was embarrassed. She had reached for something that wasn't hers. In fact – a doll belonging to the queen of Scotland!

"Mary Seton likes the blue one best," announced the little queen, "so she will play with that one."

Mary Seton had to swallow before she could speak.

"Thank you."

She forgot the doll in her hands as she watched the little girl's glowing eyes.

"I like the blue one too," the queen said, "but I like this one, too." She chose another doll. "My grandmother sent them from France. And that is where we are going."

When Viola came with her medicine, Mary pretended to drink it, then sent Viola away. She was in the bed she shared with Mary Livingston with the curtains drawn when the others entered. She lay still, listening to the others as they undressed.

"So those are the Scots nobility," Mary Livingston said. "They are not barbarians, as the French say."

"You wouldn't think so," said Mary Fleming. "You danced all evening with that man who looks like a horse and grins like an idiot."

"He does not," said Mary Livingston, "and you know it."

"Who is he?" asked Mary Beaton.

"His name is John Semple," said Mary Fleming. "And he does grin like an idiot. And he is a younger son."

"You spent all evening with a younger son," Mary Beaton teased. "How you throw away your time."

Mary Livingston pulled back the bed curtains and crawled in. When she let the curtains fall back into place, she and Mary Seton were in darkness.

"Hello," whispered Mary Seton.

"Did we wake you? I'm sorry. We heard you were ill."

"I'm all right."

"I saw Christopher Norton," Mary Livingston whispered. "I would have been sick, too! I wouldn't want to marry him! What is it about him that's so awful?"

"He's nothing. He has no thoughts of his own. He wants to marry me because I'll always have the ear of the queen of France. Our parents want us to marry because uniting the Catholics of Great Britain will please the Guises."

"Knowing your grandmother, you'll end up marrying him.

From what I understand, nobody crosses her."

"Not yet, anyway." Then: "Tell me about John Semple," she said.

"Mary Fleming doesn't like how he looks, but that's because he's a younger son. He's really very handsome. He lived in England, so they call him a 'jolly Englishman.' He's funny and he makes me laugh." As if to prove it, she giggled.

Mary Seton lay awake for a long time, wondering if Alexander Beaton would be at the celebration the following day. She wondered what she would say to him if he was. She drifted off to sleep, imagining Alexander with her by the river thickets near the convent, where the afternoon sun slanted through the branches like light in a cathedral.

She was awake before the ringing of the morning bells. She slid from the bed, careful not to awaken Mary Livingston. First she went to the far side of the room and knelt in front of the crucifix to whisper her morning prayers. Then, feeling restless and wanting to get out of the room, she dressed quickly and stepped into the corridor.

Laughter came from the Scottish queen's wardrobe room. The door was open and inside were three dress maids. When they saw Mary Seton, they stopped talking and looked at her.

"Good morning, my lady." A girl with red hair bobbed a curtsy. "Can we do something for you?"

"No, there is nothing I need." Mary Seton knew she was making them uncomfortable and that she should move on. But then she saw that one girl was holding a gold ring. From across the room, Mary could see the purple sapphire.

"Let me see that ring," Mary said.

"It's mine, my lady," said the girl, looking frightened. "A gentleman gave it to me last night."

"She's telling the truth," another girl said.

"Let me see the ring."

The girl held out the ring. The star in the sapphire was motionless in the dim light. It was the same ring that had cut into Mary's flesh the night before. She was looking at Norton's ring.

She glanced back at the girl, who was about sixteen, with very white skin and green eyes, full of fear. "A gentleman gave it to me last night, after the queen's ball. Honest, my lady."

The room was quiet enough for Mary to hear her own breath. "I believe you," she said. She turned and walked from the room. By the time she reached the back gardens, she could contain herself no longer and uttered one of the few curses she knew. "God's Nightgown! I will not marry him! I will not!"

She was glad there was no one to hear her. Finding a bench in a hidden corner of the garden, she sat for a long time, watching the sun rise over the courtyard walls.

Then she heard the sound of footsteps running up the walk. She turned to see Viola approaching, out of breath.

"Is something the matter?" Mary asked.

"Is something the matter?" Viola repeated. "You left the wedding ball last night because you were ill, and this morning I woke up to find you gone. I was worried. What did you expect?"

Mary turned away, thinking that Viola hadn't been worried about her health. Most likely, after having found Mary with Alexander the night before, Viola had been worried that when she did find Mary, she wouldn't be alone.

Viola plunked herself down on the bench beside Mary. Viola was a no-nonsense woman who always spoke her mind. She was slender, but sturdy, and thirty one years old. Her father had been a merchant from one of the Seton ports. She had married twice and had lost both husbands to the English battlefields. She had borne and buried five children, all lost to childhood diseases.

Viola's dark hair was smoothed back into a neat chignon and held in place with a thin net. She wore a loose apron tied over a russet colored garment of coarse linen. Her face was long and pointed of chin. Her dark eyes were sharp and alert.

She owed her position to her family's unwavering loyalty to the Seton clan chief.

"I will ask you again," Viola said. "Is something the matter?"

Mary shook her head no. As always she was careful to hide her thoughts from Viola, who, she suspected, reported everything she did to her family.

"Instead of sitting there staring into the sky," Viola said, "will you please tell me what's on your mind?"

"Nothing is on my mind. I wanted to walk in the garden, that's all."

"You seemed to be enjoying the ball last night. Until you suddenly and mysteriously fell ill, that is."

Mary didn't say anything. Viola always seemed know when she was lying.

"Your brother Lord Seton was pleased to see you dancing with Norton. You do know, I suppose, that Norton is the son of one of the most Catholic earls in England."

"Would it surprise you to know that he slept last night with a wardrobe maid?"

"No, it wouldn't," Viola said sharply. "But it would surprise me if you let a thing like that bother you. Why should you care what he does with serving girls?"

"I don't," said Mary, picking at a rough spot on the bench. She glanced up at the palace windows, wondering if Alexander had stayed in the palace last night.

"Viola, how did you meet your husband?"

"And why should that interest you?"

"I don't even know what his name was."

"His name was Luke. He lived in our village. I knew him from my childhood."

"Did you love him?"

Viola looked closely at Mary, her eyes hard as pebbles and narrowed with suspicion. "I had my first child before I was fifteen. I thought I loved him. I didn't know what love was, and I was a fool."

Mary stood up. "I suppose we should go in now. It is probably time for me to help the queen dress."

"I know what you want," Viola said, standing up and facing Mary squarely. "You want to defy your family and marry for love. But you are a green, foolish girl who has been pampered and indulged all your life. You know nothing of poverty or the life you would lead if you marry where there is no money."

When Mary reached the queen's private chambers, the others were already helping her into her gown. Seeing her, the queen held out her arms toward Mary Seton. "Do you feel better? We heard you'd fallen ill!"

"I'm better, thank you."

"Come, help us choose a collar piece to go with this gown."

"I think you should wear the strand of baby pearls," said Mary Fleming.

"Oh! I think so too," said Mary Beaton. "The simple, dainty pearls would be perfect with this white satin."

Mary Beaton reached into one of the queen's cabinets and took out a small silver casket. She opened it and gasped.

"What is it?" asked the queen.

Mary Beaton dug through the contents of the casket, then looked at the others, alarmed. "I know I put it in here! I shouldn't have, perhaps. This is the only casket that doesn't lock, but I was afraid the thin chain would get caught on something else!"

Mary Fleming took the casket and looked through it. "Are you sure you put it here?"

"Quite sure!" said Mary Beaton.

"Maybe it's in one of the other caskets" said one of the queen's French attendants. They all began looking through each of the queen's jewelry boxes and caskets.

"It isn't here," said the queen.

"What shall we do?" asked Mary Beaton. "If one of the

servants—"

"I will not have my wedding day spoiled," said the queen calmly. "Justice is harsh and swift and I will not have anyone accused or questioned."

"It is my responsibility," said Mary Beaton. "I am the one who put them into the casket that doesn't lock. I will replace the pearls."

"You will do nothing of the kind," said the queen. "You were right to separate that delicate chain from the others. You were also right to believe nobody would enter this cabinet without permission. It is certainly not your fault."

"But your pearls, Madam!" said someone.

The queen lifted her chin and smiled. "If someone has stolen my pearls, well, someone has grown wealthier. Today is the third day of my wedding celebrations. Today marks another celebration of my new title of dauphiness of France. Perhaps this is the Lord's way of reminding me that I have so much, and others so little. One day, many years from now, someone will boast of owning a string of pearls the queen intended to wear on the third day of her wedding festivities. We will talk no more about it – except, I think perhaps we should add a few locks to these cabinets. Mary Beaton, will you see to it? And make sure that you have the only keys."

"Yes, Madam, of course."

The Beaton family had always held the position of keeper of the Scottish crown jewels, so it was natural that the queen's jewels should be entrusted to Mary Beaton.

"And now," said the queen, "we will select a different necklace for me to wear."

*Do you see?* Mary Seton wanted to say, to nobody in particular, *do you see how generous she is, and how good and kind?*

Once the queen was dressed and ready, Mary Seton's own handmaids came to help her dress. Ordinarily she didn't care much what she wore, but this morning, after changing her mind several times, she noticed there was a great difference in how her gowns made her look. She cast away the slender-cut pink gown after deciding it made her complexion appear sallow, although it emphasized her height and slenderness. She finally decided on a pale blue gown with a delicately embroidered bodice which changed the gray of her eyes to a delicate ice-blue.

That day's celebrations were held outdoors. A pavilion of painted canvas held up by ships masts had been set up on the lawn. The canvas was decorated with painted unicorns, dragons, and lions. One platform had been built for dancing, another for the musicians. Mary Seton searched the crowds for Alexander. There were fewer people than the evening before, and she quickly concluded that he wasn't there. Or perhaps he hadn't arrived yet.

Her brother George was approaching with Christopher Norton. Both were smiling at her. The sight of Norton's glib smile made her wish she could disappear.

"I do hope you are feeling better," Norton said.

Instead of answering, she looked at Norton's hand. The ring was gone. Neither her brother nor Norton noticed her glance, but both were disturbed by her silence.

"Shall we dance, Lady Mary?" Norton asked.

She looked at him, amazed. He said, "I will pretend no cross words passed between us yesterday evening."

She smiled, which both he and George evidently took for agreement, because George said, "Good, Mary, go on." But she'd smiled because she was thinking about how Alexander Beaton would have responded to such a comment as "I will pretend no cross words passed between us."

So here she was, once again being led to the row of dancers by Christopher Norton.

The Scottish queen passed by, and the hats of every gentleman came off and the ladies swept out their skirts in deep, graceful curtseys. When the queen of Scots saw Mary

Seton, she reached over and gave her an impulsive hug. "Isn't it all so wonderful?" the queen whispered.

"Oh, it is," Mary Seton whispered back.

Once the queen passed by, the dancing resumed. The music was upbeat and lively. The curved green plume in Norton's cap swayed as they danced. When he smiled at her, she looked away.

The first chance they had to speak, Norton says, "She does favor you, doesn't she?"

"Actually, no," said Mary Seton. "I am her least favorite of the four Marys. She prefers the others to me." She enjoyed his look of discomfort. "Why?" she asked. "Have you been told otherwise?"

"I believe you are falsely modest, which is part of your charm. I must confess that you have quite bewitched me."

"You seem to have lost your ring," she said, pleased to see the smile slip from his face.

"You have sharp eyes, Lady Mary."

"Indeed," she answered.

They were separated and several minutes passed before they could speak again. "I could not stop thinking about you last night," he said, evidently deciding to ignore her reference to his ring.

"Is that why you were distracted enough to lose your ring?"

This time his expression darkened. Trying one more time, he said, "Do you doubt my love?"

"You were made to doubt."

When the dance ended and her most trusted handmaid, Annie, tapped her shoulder, Mary stepped aside to speak with her. The maid whispered, "There is a gentleman at the west gate. He asked for you."

"Thank you," she fought to keep her voice casual. "I must go," she said to Norton. Picking up her skirts, she ran off before he could stop her, ducking into the crowds so he couldn't follow. To get to the side gate, she reentered the palace and ran lightly down the marbled corridors, mostly empty now except for occasional guard wearing royal livery. She passed through a side entry way to the west gate.

Alexander was standing just outside the iron gate. As she approached, he smiled. "I had to see you again," he said. "To see if you are for real."

"What are you doing out there?"

"I wasn't invited today."

"Did you behave that badly last night?"

"My cousin thought so. I believe that younger sons can only hope for one royal invitation."

She wanted to tell him that she was glad to see him, but she seemed to have lost her ability to speak. He gripped one of the bars that separated them and gave the gate a slight shake.

"Do you have the key?" he asked.

"Do you want to come in?"

"No, I want you to come out."

"Out?" she repeated stupidly.

"Well, I certainly cannot come in without permission."

"I couldn't possibly leave." She hated to think of what would happen if she were caught outside the palace gates with Alexander Beaton, particularly now, with her brother here and Viola watching everything she did.

"Well, then, I'll have to find a way to get another invitation."

"I hope you do," she said.

"Will you wait for me?" he asked. "Will you promise not to give your heart to anyone else?"

She searched his face for signs that he was mocking her, but for once he seemed deadly serious. "I promise," she said.

"I promise as well," he said. "I will see you again soon."

During the days that followed, she moved through the routine expecting at any moment to see him. He had promised to get another invitation, and she believed that he would. Besides, there were times when the gates were opened and anyone who wished could enter limited parts of the palace – tradesmen who had goods to sell, common people petitioning the king for favors. She fully expected to see him again at any moment.

Her mind ran wild with fantasies of Alexander declaring his love for her. Her family would be furious and would refuse her a dowry, but in Mary Seton's fantasies, the beautiful and gentle queen, happy in her own marriage, would forgive Mary Seton and give her and Alexander permission to live in France, and perhaps a living as well. Why not? It happened often enough.

A week passed, and still she heard nothing from Alexander. Then her handmaid Annie brought her a note. "It came by messenger," Annie explained.

The moment Mary was alone, she broke the seal and read:

> My dear Mary: I have been ordered to leave France, as you probably know. Someone saw us together and told your brother, who appealed to the Guises and now I have been banished. You are the only real gem in the entire palace. God willing, I will see you again some day. A.B.

She wanted to find out if it had been Viola who had informed her brother about Alexander. She waited until enough time passed so that her anger wouldn't show. Then one day when Viola followed her out into the gardens, she said, "I never thought I would say this, Viola, but I am actually glad that you had Alexander Beaton sent away. When I think of all I might have given up for his sake—" she shook her head.

"I only did my duty by your family," Viola said.

Years of living at court had taught Mary Seton to hide her emotions. She was sure Viola saw nothing in her face except serenity.

She had her chance for revenge when her brother came to tell her goodbye. He and his men were ready to return to Scotland. "Mary," he said, "before I leave I want your word that you will marry Christopher Norton when the time comes."

She swallowed. With luck, the negotiations could take many months. In the meantime, she would have plenty of time to talk to the queen to see if she could help her find a way out of the marriage. Her brother might force her to marry a man she despised, but the queen would not. Wouldn't it be a nice irony if her favor with the queen helped her avoid the marriage, when it was her favor with the queen which made her a desirable wife?

Because, for now, she had no choice, she said, "Yes, George, you know that I will."

He kissed her forehead. "You have always been a dutiful sister and an honor to our family."

"George, I have a favor to ask. I no longer want Viola in my service."

George eyed her sharply. "Why? Viola has always been faithful."

"It is my wish."

"Are you angry with Viola because she has done the duty we have assigned her?"

"I am not angry with Viola."

George was still studying her. Thank goodness she was practiced at hiding her emotions. This was her only power.

"Very well, Mary. You seldom ask for anything. Since you have agreed to the marriage, you shall have your wish. If Viola has somehow offended you, I shall bring her back with me to Scotland."

"Thank you," Mary said. She knew that Viola, who loved living at the French court, would be hurt and disappointed. But Mary no longer wanted Viola near her. Having Viola banished from the French Court was the only act of revenge Mary Seton ever committed.

# Destiny

# INTERLUDE
# FOTHERINGAY CASTLE

"After the queen's wedding in Paris," Clare said, "that was when the queen's troubles began. Right?"

"Oh, goodness no," said Mary Seton. "The two years following the queen's wedding were the happiest of her life. The wedding elevated her rank. She was now married to the heir to all of France, and was called queen-dauphiness. Poets sang her praises. The people adored her. Some who were cynical said, well why *shouldn't* the people adore her? After all, she brought an independent kingdom in her dowry."

"And what about you? What were those years like for you?"

Mary Seton grew quiet and looked toward the window. The glass was frosted and heavily leaded, too thick to see outside, but glossy enough to reflect the candlelight, and Mary's face.

"During those years," Lady Mary said quietly, "I felt that I was waiting for something. I was young, so perhaps I felt I was waiting for my life to begin. With my queen elevated so high, I felt nothing was impossible."

"But what was it *like* to live in a French royal palace?"

"It was like living in a well-organized, well-regulated political institution."

"Were there always lots of people around?"

"Always, lots. For those like Mary Fleming or even the queen, who wanted to be surrounded by people all the time, it was like heaven itself. In the king's private household alone, there were six hundred members including confessors, doctors, surgeons, apothecaries, barbers, stewards, gentlemen and ladies of the chambers, valets, bread carriers, cup bearers, and on and on. We saw the king at ten o'clock each day for Mass, and often during late afternoon games or tournaments. Twice each week he held a ball. The queen had her own separate household, as did the queen of Scotland and the dauphin. Then, when the King died, and her husband became king of France, we all moved into the most sumptuous apartments in the palace."

"I cannot imagine it!" said Clare.

"There were also painters and artists and poets. The artisans were the best in all of Europe. Even before she became queen of France, the Scottish queen was the centerpiece, and the focus of so much excitement and happiness. Through her, the Guise family was about to ascend to the highest honor in the kingdom."

"Did the queen really love her husband?"

"Oh, she did. He adored her. I think there were only two people on earth her husband truly loved – his mother, and the queen of Scots. But remember, they were children when they married, after all, and he died so young."

This part of the story Clare knew, because everyone knew it: The one year after the queen's wedding to the dauphin, the king of France died of an infection when a lance splintered and entered his eye. The dauphin and queen of Scots were crowned king and queen of France. But ten months later, the young king – only sixteen years old – died of an infection in his ear.

"What a shock it must have been when he died!"

"He had always been sickly and weak. And there were omens, of course."

"Omens?"

"The plague, the black death, had not touched Europe for many years, but during the winter of 1559 an epidemic spread over England and parts of Scotland. That was also the year the queen of Scots made an enemy of her cousin Elizabeth of England.

"Was that when the troubles began?"

"The troubles began shortly after we all returned to Scotland."

# CHAPTER 2

A flourish of trumpets marked Scottish queen's entry into Edinburgh. The people of Edinburgh, who had not seen their queen since she was a child of five, had set up a rose-garnished triumphal arch to welcome her. The twisted, dusty streets were packed with thousands of cheering townspeople. A chorus of bells rang, and banners of red, blue, and gold waved from the red sandstone houses.

The queen, wearing mourning robes of black for her late husband, rode in the first carriage with her uncle the Duke of Guise. Mary Seton rode in the second carriage with the other Marys. They made a sweet picture in their French court gowns trimmed with pale silk, fastened back to display richly embroidered kirtles and petticoats, looking as much alike as four roses cut from the same branch.

"We should not have come back," Mary Beaton said. "I tried to warn her. It's too dangerous. There is no law here anymore."

"But look at them," said Mary Livingston. "I think their welcome is sincere. And I'm glad to be back."

"You would be," said Mary Beaton. "All you care about is seeing your Jolly Englishman again. You don't have enough sense to be afraid of the rebels."

Mary Seton scanned the crowds, hoping to catch sight of Alexander Beaton. During the three years since the queen's wedding, she often wondered if her fantasies had transformed him to a hero beyond anyone she could possibly recognize. Whenever courtiers had tried to flatter her or her family wrote to her about Christopher Norton, she had remembered Alexander Beaton and her promise that she would never give her heart to anyone else. He had promised the same. She wondered what he was doing now and whether he had kept his promise.

The streets were dark from the overhanging upper stories. Pearl-gray pigeons fluttered around the crow-stepped gables. The streets were so crowded it was difficult for the royal procession to pass through.

In an open square, a group of children performed a play in the Scottish queen's honor. They sang praises to their 'beloved new Kirk' – the Scottish word for 'church,'

Mary Seton was shocked. "Do they mean it?" she asked.

"Of course not," Mary Livingston said. But Mary Seton wasn't sure any more what to believe. The queen's uncle the Duke of Guise said that Protestantism had been forced on the Scottish people by lying rebels. He'd insisted that the Scots were still loyal Catholics at heart and would welcome the chance to return to the true religion.

But then the actors on the stage parted and a boy stepped forward, wearing the fur-trimmed mantle and woolen tartan of the Argyle clan. He bowed to the queen and handed her a bouquet of white roses. "In the name of God," the boy said, "I beg you to set aside the idolatrous Mass and icons of the false and wicked Church of Rome and accept our new kirk—"

"They do mean it," Mary Beaton whispered.

Mary Beaton's family was one of the few in Scotland more staunchly Catholic than the Setons. Most of the Beaton wealth had been connected with the church. Mary Beaton's uncle the Cardinal Beaton had been murdered during the Reformation, and her other uncle, the Archbishop Beaton, had fled to France. Of the four Marys, only Mary Beaton had not wanted to return.

The queen gave the reply her uncles had advised: "I cannot turn away from the church of my fathers," she told the child. "But I will not upset the present religion in Scotland. In return I demand the right to follow my own religion in private."

The crowd burst into shouts and applause. How could they not when the queen responded so graciously? The queen waved at the cheering crowds, smiling sweetly, her face flushed prettily. The simply cut gown she wore emphasized her extraordinary height, making her look positively regal. Mary Seton, listening, thought that the people here would love her, as the French had. It might take time to overcome the mistrust and suspicions because, after all, she and her people were strangers to each other, but Mary Seton had no doubt that the Scottish queen could win their trust.

The carriages continued down High Street to Holyrood Palace. The palace entryway was flanked by two square masonry towers. Just inside was an open cobblestone courtyard. Holyrood Palace loomed above, its dark crenellated battlements topped with turrets.

Mary Seton stepped down from the carriage and felt a light tap on her shoulder.

"Welcome home, Mary."

She whirled around. "George!" He kissed her half-brother's cheek and spontaneously hugged him, forgetting that the last time she had seen him in France she had considered him more an enemy than a brother. "I'm glad to be back, George."

"You won't be glad for long when you find out what a hotbed of trouble you've come to. Two weeks ago, churches were still burning. We've just put out the last of the fires."

"Was it as bad as they say?"

"Worse."

It couldn't have been worse then some of the stories she'd heard of the brutal and fierce Scots, still crudely medieval in their ways of thinking, with the people pledging their greatest allegiance to their clan chief instead of the sovereign.

"Come," George said, leading her to waiting horses. "I will take you to the townhouse. Our grandmother wishes to see you."

They rode through the streets which were still crowded with townspeople carrying welcoming flags and banners. At the wynd-post of the Seton Townhouse, a stable boy waited to take their horses.

Mary's grandmother sat near the window of the main hall. She remembered her grandmother cradling her as a child, telling her stories of her illustrious ancestors. Her grandmother had made her learn the responses of the Mass by heart, long before she knew what the words meant.

"Come here, Mary," her grandmother commanded.

Mary crossed the room and kissed her grandmother's cheek. Her grandmother smelled of verbena.

"I hoped to welcome you home under happier conditions," her grandmother said briskly. "But we are all proud of you, Mary."

"I have done nothing."

"But you have. We received constant reports. At all times you conducted yourself with the reserve and pride befitting a Seton."

Mary considered telling her grandmother what her life had been like at the French court. Surely her grandmother would understand that she had hated the lies and malicious gossip and constant intriguing of the courtiers.

But her grandmother went on, "There is no need to worry about these present troubles. We Catholics are making plans. Even if the queen doesn't marry the Spanish prince, there are other ways beat the Protestants. We can unite the Catholics of

Scotland and England."

"Grandmother, to talk of politics so soon—"

"I am talking about your future bridegroom." The harsh lines of her grandmother's face softened. "I believe you have met Christopher Norton."

"Yes, grandmother. He was at the queen's wedding in Paris."

"He is a fine young man. And I don't have to tell you who his father is. They are loyal Catholics, pledged to putting down these rebels."

"But it is too early to speak of my marriage. The queen is still unmarried, and may be for many months."

"It is not too early for us to make our plans. I am pleased with the marriage being arranged for you. When I see the last of my grandchildren married, I can die in peace."

"But grandmother, I don't think I could love Christopher Norton."

"Love is no reason to marry. The saying goes, 'carnal marriages begin in happiness and end in strife. A girl must marry for the good of her family. Every Seton has done so."

Mary stood silently, the picture of meek obedience, as her grandmother talked about their marriage plans. She felt the familiar coldness spreading inside her. She knew it would do no good to try to talk to her.

"I will keep you informed of our negotiations," her grandmother said. Mary told herself that there was no sense in making a scene yet. For now, at least, there was only one answer to give: "Yes, grandmother."

Defeated, Mary Seton returned to Holyrood Palace. Her mother and George's wife  Isabelle came to Holyrood Palace that night to greet her, but Mary fared no better with them. They talked in the queen's antechamber, a large room with comfortable chairs. Like George and her grandmother, they only wanted to talk about her honor at the French Court and her coming marriage to Christopher Norton. Mary had never before met her sister-in-law Isabelle. Talking to them was like talking to strangers. Mary Seton was polite and gracious – and happy when they left.

When they were gone, a serving girl led Mary Seton to her new room, a chamber adjoining the queen's private rooms. Compared to the spacious and luxurious French palaces, Holyrood was dark and cramped. As at the French court, she would share this room with the other three Marys. Her wooden trunk and was looking through its contents of kirtles, caps, and stockings was there, having been sent from France.

Annie, her handmaid, entered and said, "My lady, there is a gentleman at the side gate for you."

Mary stood up and thanked the girl. She had no doubt who was at the gate. In that moment it seemed as if it had been just yesterday when Alexander had sent for her from the gates of the French palace.

She picked up her skirts and hurried to the side gate. She found him standing alone. He was taller than she remembered, at least three inches taller than her, and she stood higher than all but the tallest men. His hair was longer, thicker, and darker than she remembered, but it still curled softly about his neck. She felt suddenly weak. He was everything she had remembered, and more.

Very simply, as if no time at all had passed, he said, "Hello, Mary."

"Hello."

"So you remember me?"

"Of course I remember you. I made you a promise. I never forget promises."

"I made you more than one promise. I promised I would get another invitation to the court, but I couldn't." He gripped the iron of the gate separating them.

"I believe you would be permitted in today," she said. "With so many people coming to welcome the queen, even an outspoken younger son would be allowed in."

"I was invited tonight, for the dancing," he said. "But I

wanted to talk to you first. I won't be able to speak to you tonight, as I'd like, and I was afraid you would think I had forgotten you."

"Why won't you be able to talk to me?" Then she remembered. Her brother had banished him from the French Court. "My brother will be there," she said.

"I still want you to come out," he said.

She drew in her breath. Did she dare? She wanted to venture out of the palace gates, desperately. She had never done anything like that before. And here was Alexander, beckoning to her, as he had done so many times in her daydreams.

The last time he'd asked, she'd been three years younger, and so much had happened since then, and so much had changed it was staggering. "Maybe I will," she said.

"Good," he said. "Sunday, after Mass, when the court is quiet, I'll meet you down the Cannongate, on the next corner," he pointed toward the heart of Edinburgh.

Was it as easy as that?

Just before the court ball that evening, a red rose arrived for Mary Livingston with a note that she wouldn't let anyone see. The other Marys gathered around her.

"It's from the Jolly Englishman," said Mary Beaton.

"'Jolly' is a polite way to describe him," said Mary Fleming. When Mary Livingston flushed happily, Mary Fleming said, "You should not be this excited about a younger son. Younger sons have nothing."

"What do I care about that?" asked Mary Livingston

Mary Seton looked on, enviously, wishing her family was more like the Livingstons, less grand and less ambitious.

When the queen's mother, Mary of Guise, reigned as Queen of Scotland, she'd done much to transform Holyrood Palace, which had been built centuries before as a monastery, into a French style Palace. She brought pear and plum trees for the orchards, wild boars for hunting, and lush tapestries and fine paintings. The Holyrood Palace ballroom was paneled richly with wood, and the floors laid with real carpet instead of rushes.

Alexander Beaton was at the ball, with several of his clansmen. Mary Seton looked at him whenever she dared, and twice he smiled at her. She watched Mary Livingston dancing with John Semple, wishing that she could dance with Alexander. But her brother was standing nearby, and she was not yet ready to create a scene with her family.

On Sunday after Mass, Mary Seton stood alone in her room in front of a mirror of burnished bronze. She wore a simple beige muslin gown such as a village girl might wear to church. She put a veil over her hair and a plain shawl over her shoulders.

Picking up her skirts and keeping her head lowered, she ran down the corridor to one of the side gates.

Alexander was standing in a corner of the first open square, waiting for her. She took off her veil and smiled.

"Did you have trouble getting away?" he asked.

"None at all."

He took her hand and they walked down the crowded Cannongate, away from Holyrood. Was this really her walking hand in hand with Alexander Beaton? She felt she was living one of her fantasies. She kept looking up at him, and once, when she caught him watching her, she flushed, embarrassed, and looked away. She felt trembly and warm inside. She wanted to say something, but she couldn't think of a single thing to say.

On the streets, going about their business, were other girls her age, some carrying baskets, others carrying infants, still others carrying wares they were selling. No wonder the queen and the dauphin had so enjoyed their adventures dressing up and sneaking out of the palace to roam the streets of Paris. How free she felt now! How exhilarating to be completely anonymous, to blend into the crowds, not to be watched or whispered about.

Alexander said, "What would the mighty Setons say if they knew where you were right now?"

"Don't even ask," she said. "I don't like to think about it."

They found a grassy spot to sit where the Cowgate turned into the narrow Candlemaker Road. They could see down the hill, past the marshes, all the way to the Firth of Forth. The cowslip, the marsh marigold, was in full bloom and the purple heather was just coming out.

A few tradesmen passed by wearing the Seton plaid of bold green, red, and narrow stripes of navy. There was little chance of anyone recognizing her, but she kept her face averted.

"I've heard a few rumors about you," Alexander said. "I've heard your family is arranging a marriage with Christopher Norton. The man you told me was 'nobody.'"

"As far as I'm concerned, he is nobody. I will not marry him."

Alexander looked at her, curious. "Have you told your family that yet?"

Some of the bravado went out of her voice when she said, "No, not yet."

He was still holding her hand. She let her hand rest in his, afraid to look into his face. Then he told her about how his family was trying to force him to go to the continent and become a priest. It was a tradition that younger Beaton sons entered the church, and now that the Reformation in Scotland had made it impossible, this was their idea.

"Will you go?" she asked.

"No."

She looked at him. "Have you told your family that yet?"

He smiled. "They have been trying to their best to get me to go, but so far I have held out. I am hoping that soon they will give up."

"How are they trying to get you to go?"

"By pointing out that I have no alternatives. They say my only other choice is to find and marry an heiress."

For one horrible moment she wondered if Alexander thought she was heiress to the Seton fortunes. Years of living at the French court had made her wary and suspicious. Then she recovered. He couldn't possibly think she was heiress. He could, however, think she had a sizable dowry.

So she said, "My former governess never tired of telling me that I'll be left penniless if I refuse to marry as my brother commands."

"Does that frighten you?" he asked.

She smiled. "Not at all."

Before long the sun was low in the sky. How different the long, softly-lit afternoons were here, in this far northern region. Indeed there was a charm in the lingering Scottish afternoons when the feeble, blood-red sun, crept to the horizon. She liked how the hills north of the town looked in the warm hazy light, so different from the bright sunny skies of France.

Alexander said, "It's too bad you're the daughter of the Sixth Premier Baron of Scotland."

"Why?" she asked, her heart beating faster.

"It does create certain complications, you must admit."

What complications, she wanted to know. Instead of asking, she said, "I cannot tell you how many times I've wished that I were not the daughter of the Sixth Premier Baron of Scotland. I've often wished I could escape."

"I know," he said. "I've wished for that, too. We are supposed to simply accept that our destines are set by the circumstances of our births." A moment later, he added, "I suppose most people's destines are determined at birth."

The chill of evening was coming into the air. "I should go back now," she said.

"When can you come out again?"

"You want to see me again? Even if I am the daughter of the Sixth Premier Baron of Scotland?"

"It would be easier if you were a common village girl," he said.

Lifting her chin and summoning her courage, she said, "What would be easier?"

"Seeing you as often as I'd like. Can you come out again next Sunday?"

"I'll try," she said.


She met him the following Sunday, and the Sunday after that. Their days were pleasant, free from court intrigue, free from tension. She lived each week for the time she would find him waiting for her at the gate.

Four weeks after their first meeting, she told him that the Seton Castle was being reopened now that her brother had finished the renovations. Her brother was holding a masked ball to celebrate. "I wish I could arrange an invitation for you without making my family suspicious," she told him.

"Maybe I can sneak in, masked. If someone does recognize me, they'll suppose I came with my cousin."

"All right," she said, thinking of her stern grandmother, "but if you get caught, I will deny having anything to do with it."

"My dear Mary," he said, "you are a coward."

She smiled. "Maybe I am."


The following day, she traveled to the Seton estates in East Lothian with her mother, George's wife Isabelle, two of the younger of her half-brothers, and their wives. The East Lothian hills were covered with a profusion of the fragrant cowslip. Herds of cattle grazed over the clover-filled meadows tended by the sons of nearby cottagers. Each of the Seton villages through which they passed was a tangle of dusty streets lined with cottages thatched with dried heather. When the villagers learned that Lord Seton's family was passing through, they came out to greet them. Mary was startled by their enthusiastic cheers as they ran up from the fields and shouted and waved.

"They are proud of all they have heard of you, Mary," her

mother said. "They are proud that you are lady-in-waiting to the queen."

Isabelle added, "And when they hear of the marriage we are arranging for you, they will be prouder still."

Mary felt the familiar cold anger come over her. These villagers, who she didn't know, expected her to make a state marriage, just as her family expected it. She felt that she was owned, body and soul, by strangers.

At last the gray towers of the castle appeared in the distance. Through a wide gate in the outer masonry walls, they passed through a large open grounds designed as a tournament ring. Next came a series of gate towers pierced with narrow slits through which archers could aim at an attacking army. Alongside the main gate tower hung a heavy metal gong. Before the gong could be sounded, three squires came forward to take their horses.

Mary was taken through a vaulted chamber to the stairway which led to the living quarters. The chamber was lined with displays of ancient Seton armorial bearings and full suits of armor, some many centuries old. The castle, which had been built as a fortress, was smaller and darker than she remembered. In France, the ruins of old moat-encircled castles were scattered about the countryside, relics of a feudal past. But in Scotland, the constant warfare between the clans demanded the upkeep of military castles.

Mary's room was dominated by a curtained bed and a large hooded fireplace. A chest lay at the foot of her bed, and a set of cupboards were dug into the thickness of the wall. The latticed casements and protective iron grille of the room's only window cast a diamond pattern over the bare stone floors. She could peer through the window's iron grille to the hills that stretched to the horizon. She had been happy to return to Scotland, but she felt as much a stranger here as she had at the French court.

On the night of the ball, Mary Beaton arrived with the

latest court gossip: one of the Protestants who had led the rebellion, William Maitland, was courting Mary Fleming and hoped to marry her.

"She'll never marry him," Mary Livingston said. "She'd never marry a Protestant. Never."

Mary Seton, remembering Mary Fleming's flirtation with Henri, the Prince of Conde's cousin, thought otherwise. "She won't marry him," said Mary Seton, "but not because he's Protestant. She won't marry him because he's old, a commoner, and has no wealth."

Mary Beaton said. "You've been away from the court for the past week, so you haven't heard the news. Their romance is the greatest joke in Edinburgh. Everyone says Maitland is as fit to be her husband as Queen Elizabeth is fit to be the Pope."

As if to prove the rumors true, Mary Fleming entered the ballroom holding Maitland's arm.

"What does the queen say?" Mary Seton asked Mary Beaton.

"She says she will approve of whatever will make her cousin happy."

"Unbelievable," Mary Seton murmured. But on second thought, it was perfectly believable. The queen would naturally trust Mary Fleming. It would never occur to her that someone who she loves might do something to hurt her.

"Soon we will all be married," said Mary Livingston. "Imagine that. As soon as the queen remarries, which she is sure to do soon, each of us will get married as well."

"You'll marry John Semple," Mary Beaton said, "and Mary Seton will marry Christopher Norton. Mary Fleming might just marry Maitland. What about me, I wonder? I don't have Mary Seton's dowry, so I cannot hope for someone as grand as Christopher Norton."

Mary Seton didn't respond. So they all took it for granted that she would marry Norton. How surprised they would be when she didn't.

Sometime later, when Mary Seton was standing alone, someone tapped her arm. "You had better warn the guards," Alexander whispered. "I heard rumor that an unworthy younger son has slipped in looking for the grand Lady Mary Seton."

"In ten minutes," she whispered, amazed by her own boldness, "meet me on the upstairs balcony."

He nodded and lost himself in the crowd of dancers.

She dutifully talked with her brother and then briefly joined the line of dancers. When no one was looking, she made her way upstairs to the balcony. Alexander was sitting in a darkened corner on a carved wooden bench. She sat beside him. They had never been alone this way. Always during their walks through Edinburgh they had been surrounded by crowds.

She sat still, waiting, wondering what he would do. After a few awkward moments, he reach for her hands and pulled her closer. She sat so near him she could feel his shoulder against hers. When he turned to talk to her, she felt his breath near her cheek.

He tipped her chin up and kissed her. Sitting in darkness with his arms around her and his lips on hers made her forget everything except his nearness. She could smell the starch in his ruff and she could feel the silk of his doublet beneath her hands. From far away she heard the beat of the music, but it came to her more as a rhythm than a melody, a beat she felt in the vibrations of the floor matching her own heartbeat.

When he dropped his head to kiss her throat, she felt frightened by the pleasure she felt. How gentle yet exciting his kisses were. She wanted to move even closer to him and press against him, but fear took over.

"I wonder sometimes," he said, "if you can really prefer me to the eldest son of an earl. He can offer you so much more."

"I don't want anything from Christopher Norton."

When he squeezed her hand, she said, "It's too bad I'm

not heiress to the Seton fortunes."

"If you were," he said, lifting her hand and kissing it, "I couldn't marry you. I'd be afraid to make my family that happy."

The teasing note was back in his voice. She smiled into the darkness. "And I would have to wonder if you wanted me for my fortune. But if I marry without my family's permission, I'd be as poor as a barefoot village girl."

"I think I'd like you that way," he said. "Barefoot."

"It won't be easy for us to marry. My family will never approve."

"If the queen gives us permission," he said, "would your family still object?"

"I'm afraid that even with the queen's permission there would be an uproar worse than the Reformation."

He laughed quietly. "Is your grandmother as frightening as all that?"

"Worse. I don't think anyone has ever defied her. She certainly doesn't expect it of me, who she believes to be the most docile and obedient of her grandchildren."

She rested her head against his shoulder, content to feel his arms around her.

Then came the unexpected sound of the castle gates clanking open.

From the balcony she and Alexander could hear shouts from inside. George was giving orders for fresh horses to be brought from the stables.

"Something has happened," Mary said.

Below, someone shouted, "A gang of Protestant rebels destroyed the queen's private church and injured her priest!"

"I'd better go," said Alexander.

"Yes," she said.

"I will see you again," he said, "as soon as I can."

She sat alone, in the darkness, after he left. She could hear enough of what was being said below to know that the

Bothwell and Hamilton clans were feuding in the streets. Bothwell was Protestant and Hamilton was Catholic.

The following day, she returned to Holyrood to find the palace in an uproar. Her brother had gathered an army from the Seton lands and joined two other Catholic lords, who marched into Edinburgh to defend the queen.

Because of all the fighting, two weeks passed before she could meet Alexander again. This time when she met him on the Cannongate, he had two horses with him. They rode out through the low hills just southwest of Edinburgh. It was early autumn and the heather was in full bloom, covering the distant hills in velvety purple. The road was muddy from the recent rains. From atop Bonaly Hill, they could see all the way to the Firth of Forth. The gray towers of Edinburgh Castle high on Castle Rock crowned the city. In the late afternoon shadows, the light played tricks on the white birches, turning them purple. Crossing a creek on a bridge that was nothing more than a dozen boards and a broken handrail, they passed through a tiny village which consisted of a handful of thatched cottages clustered around a courtyard and small white-washed kirk.

"Did you know," said Alexander, "that the marriage laws in Scotland are the most lax in Europe. For a man and a woman to marry here all they have to do is exchange promises in front of a witness and they are legally married. Young people do not even need their parent's consent."

"Those are not the laws that apply to us, I'm afraid."

"No, I suppose not."

Members of the nobility needed the queen's consent to marry because too often marriages were used to solidify family power which might threaten the crown. And if she married without her family's permission, she would be left destitute. Besides, laws were one thing, but Lord George Seton was powerful enough to bend the law to suit his will. Should Alexander marry Seton's sister without permission, there would be little to protect Alexander against George's wrath.

On their way back, Alexander broke off a twig of thistle and handed it to her. She tucked it into her waistband and smiled at him.

When they returned to the Cannongate, he said, "I don't know when I will be leaving," he said, "but I have received orders from my uncle the Archbishop that I must journey to Rome on business for him."

"When will you be back?" she asked.

"Some time during the winter. I only agreed to go because it will be months before the queen decides on a husband. You and I cannot possibly marry until the queen remarries, and I can't afford to anger my uncle right now. He is powerful, Mary, and can help us if he chooses."

He helped her down from her horse and kissed her goodbye. "I'll hurry back," he said. "I promise. And I'll try to see you before I go."


A few weeks passed with no word from him. When a few more weeks went by, she asked one of Mary Beaton's housemaids and learned that he had already left for Italy. There was nothing she could do now except wait for him to come back.

One day, in a nostalgic mood, she took her pewter casket from her wardrobe. The casket locked with a key and in it she kept the two notes Alexander had written her on his way to the continent, and a miniature portrait of him. Inside also was the bit of thistle he had given her when they had gone riding. The moment she took the casket from the shelf, she knew something was wrong. The lock was bent as if someone had forced it open. She could see that her letters had been folded differently than she folded them.

"God's Nightgown!" she whispered. Whoever had gone through her letters knew the truth about her and Alexander.

She waited for the worst, expecting at any moment to be summoned to her grandmother, but days passed and nobody said anything. She threw all of Alexander's letters into the large hooded fireplace in the queen's antechamber. She hated to burn his letters, but it was too dangerous to keep them. The portrait, a treasure she was lucky to have, she hid among her mementos of her family where she hoped it would escape detection.

She spent as much time as she dared in Holyrood's chapel, the one place where she could be completely alone. She loved the chapel, which was lit by candles set in latticed casements of colored glass.

When she wasn't hiding in the chapel, she was forced to listen to the court gossip, which was, just then, about the queen's marriage negotiations. Would the queen marry the Catholic prince of Spain? Or would she marry King Eric of Sweden? Or would she marry the son of Lord Hamilton, the most powerful clan chief in Scotland? Mary Seton found that the constant talk about marriage made waiting for Alexander much more difficult.

More and more Scottish families were converting to Protestantism, including the Flemings and the Livingstons. Mary Fleming converted along with her family and often attended Protestant sermons. Mary Seton couldn't help feeling that Mary Fleming was betraying the queen, who would never renounce Catholicism. Mary Livingston evidently felt the same way: when her family converted, she remained Catholic to show her loyalty to the queen.

One day, Mary Fleming and Maitland were planning to attend a Protestant sermon. Mary Fleming invited the other Marys to join her.

"Do not even talk to me about Protestant sermons," Mary Beaton said. "One of my uncles was murdered by the Protestants and the other had to flee to France. Everything our family owns was destroyed by those murderers. Do not even mention them to me," she said, and stalked from the room.

"Will you go?" Mary Fleming asked Mary Livingston.

"What will the queen think if we all start attending Protestant sermons?" Mary Livingston demanded.

Mary Fleming said, "The queen herself proclaimed Protestantism the official religion of the realm."

"That is only because she has no choice," Mary Livingston said.

Mary Fleming said, "The queen is holding on to old-fashioned attitudes that are changing all over Europe."

Mary Seton listened, suspecting that Mary Fleming was repeating words which she had heard from someone else, probably Maitland. When Mary Livingston insisted that they had to remain Catholic to show loyalty to the queen, Mary Fleming gave up and turned to Mary Seton. "Will you come?"

"I am afraid not."

"And why not?" asked Mary Fleming.

"Do you have any idea what my grandmother would say if I went to a Protestant sermon and she found out?"

"Ah, yes," said Maitland. "Your grandmother, the grand old lady of Seton, as stern and formidable as ever was any matriarch."

"My grandmother takes her responsibilities seriously."

"I am sure she does," said Maitland. "Will you never have the courage to stand up to her?"

"Good question," said Mary Fleming. "Where is the kind of spirit our queen admires?"

Mary Livingston said, "Our queen admires spirit, but she does not admire treachery."

"Do you know what I think?" said Mary Fleming, ignoring Mary Livingston. "I think Mary Seton has plenty of spunk. Nobody can be as controlled as she is and be weak at heart. She's just hiding her spunk, that's all, but one day she'll surprise everyone. One day she'll tell her grandmother to go to the devil, and I hope I'm there!"

January turned to February and February turned to March,

and for months Mary Seton heard nothing from Alexander. The coming of spring was in the air. A transparent green veil hung over the tangled ivy, but the winds were still icy. One morning in mid-March she was awake before the others and decided that a walk in the palace gardens was worth braving the morning air. She bundled herself in a heavy woolen cloak and tucked her hands into a fur muff.

As she slipped into the corridor, a serving girl drew her aside. "Lady Mary," she said. "I have a letter for you." The girl pressed sealed envelope into her hand. Mary thanked her and slipped out the door. Not until she was in the far reaches of the garden, sitting on a bench with her back to the palace walls did she break the seal.

She knew it was from Alexander. As she skimmed the few lines, she went colder than the winds that swept across the bare gardens.

> My Dearest Mary: I'm sorry I couldn't write to you sooner. It was hard enough to get this letter to you since I have no money to use for bribery. Also I wanted to wait until I could find out why I have been detained in Rome. I am all but a prisoner here, being denied means for travel. Somehow your brother found out about us and has contacted the Archbishop my uncle, which is why I was called to Italy. My uncle refuses to hear my pleas. I am being held here until you are married to Norton. My only choices are to take priestly vows or marry someone of my uncle's choice. Oh, Mary, had I suspected any of this, I would never have left Scotland. Please forgive me. A.B.

It seemed several minutes before she remembered to breathe. Had her heart not gone on beating of its own accord, she was sure she would never have breathed again.

When she recovered enough, her first coherent thought was that she would speak to the queen immediately. Only the queen could overrule George's hateful actions.

But the queen was having troubles of her own. A band of Protestant rebels again attacked her private chapel and this time her priest was murdered. She ordered the ringleaders to trial. The trial, however, was a shambles. The Protestant lords in her kingdom were too powerful and Parliament declared the rebels innocent. "It cannot be proven that these are the guilty men," they declared.

In her privy chambers with her Marys, she said, "My own subjects are rebelling against me and I am powerless to punish them. The King of Spain, my only hope, is twisted around the hand of the Protestant queen Elizabeth of England! What can I do?"

Mary Seton could see plain enough that the queen wouldn't be able to free Alexander from Rome. She had no authority in her own realm. What power would she have on the continent? Still she waited until the time was right to ask the queen for help. "Of course I will write a letter on behalf of your friend," the queen said.

The queen indeed wrote the letter, that very evening. Mary spent the weeks, then months, following waiting and hoping for a change. Eventually she was forced to acknowledge the queen's letter did no good. If the Duke of Guise wanted the Setons to ally themselves with the Nortons, the queen's letter could easily be dismissed as sweet and sentimental, but not practical. And after all, it was unlikely those in Rome wanted to offend George Seton, one of the few remaining champions of Catholicism in Scotland. Unlike the queen of Scots, he could gather and lead an army to fight for Catholicism.

Mary Seton was filled with loathing and fury at her brother. Had she once loved him? Now it seemed impossible. As a child he had taken care of her and comforted her, but now she was a pawn in his political maneuvering. But her brother had a surprise coming. She wouldn't marry Christopher Norton and that was all. If she had to take religious vows and become a nun, she would. But she'd never marry Christopher Norton. Never.

The chief question on everyone's mind was who the queen would marry. She'd now given up on the negotiations with Spain. She had no wish to marry her other suitors – the archduke Charles of Austria, while Catholic, had little else to offer.

One of the queen's ambitions was to have her cousin Elizabeth Tudor recognize her as her heir should she never marry and have children. To that end, she wanted to marry with Queen Elizabeth's approval.

One day, Elizabeth sent word that she had a suggestion for the Scottish queen's next husband, the perfect bridegroom. She hinted that should the queen of Scots marry as she suggested, she would name her heiress. The Scottish queen dispatched her ambassador, Melville, at once to the English court to find out who Elizabeth thought she should marry.

Three days later, Melville returned.

"Well?" the queen demanded. "Who does my cousin think I should marry."

Melville cleared his throat. "Madam, the queen of England has made a startling suggestion, and I am not entirely comfortable bringing you her message."

"Now, Melville, how startling can it be? You have had three days to get used to the idea."

"Madam, she suggests that you marry Robert Dudley."

"Dudley? Her horse master?"

Robert Dudley was the son of a duke executed for treason. He was the man Queen Elizabeth was said to be in love with.

"The queen of England insults me," she said.

"Because he is the man she has been in love with for years, she probably does not consider it an insult. And because, for some time now, Dudley has considered himself on the verge of marrying Queen Elizabeth and therefore a step away from the English throne, I am certain Dudley doesn't think it an insult."

"I am an anointed queen of Scotland and married queen of France. I am descended from Henry VII of England. I can have my choice of the crowned heads of Europe. And the queen of England suggests that I marry her horse master, who is not even of noble rank?"

"The queen of England considered that you might object to his low rank. Therefore, she has promoted him to the rank of earl. Dudley is now the Earl of Leicester."

The queen was staring at Melville. "Are you sure she is serious?"

"Quite sure. At first, though, I was so sure she was joking, I suggested she marry Dudley herself and leave you heiress to both her kingdom and her husband."

The queen's sense of humor got the better of her, and she actually smiled. "If she is in love with him, why should she send him to Scotland to marry me?"

"I have given that question some thought, Madam, and the more I think about it, the better I understand the English queen's reasoning. She knows she cannot marry Dudley – er, she cannot marry the Earl of Leicester – without losing authority in her realm. But she trusts him as she trusts few others. She is convinced he would be a safe husband for you because he is Protestant, and he would never enter any policies which would endanger her or England."

"If the queen of England cannot marry the Earl of Leicester without losing her authority, what makes her think I can?"

You are the unquestioned queen of Scotland. Her position as Queen of England, as you know, is not as secure."

"It is a preposterous suggestion," said the queen.

"It is quite eccentric."

"What does Dudley say about all of this?"

"He isn't saying much. Like you, he has his eye on the English throne. If she never marries, you will most likely inherit her throne as her nearest kin. But Dudley – er, I mean the Earl of Leicester – sees a quicker way to become King of England, namely marry Queen Elizabeth."

Two weeks later, before Queen Mary gave an official answer to Queen Elizabeth's suggestion, Queen Elizabeth granted permission for Lord Dudley, the son of the countess of Lennox, to journey to Scotland to pay respects to the Scottish queen.

The countess of Lennox, like the Queen of Scots, was descended from King Henry VII of England. Darnley, therefore, like the queen of Scots, was in line to the English throne.

Darnley was unquestionably handsome, his features finely chiseled and delicate. He made an ostentatious display of finery with heavy jeweled rings and gold-fringed brocades. To everyone's surprise, the queen seemed to fall instantly in love with him. "He is the best looking young man I have ever seen," she exclaimed. Every day they went riding together, and every night they danced together. When the queen was not around, Darnley swaggered around, his head high and haughty, his chest puffed up. He wanted to do nothing other than hunt and hawk and boast of his flirtation with the queen of Scots.

Mary Queen of Scots was ready to marry again. Months and months passed, and nothing came of any of her marriage negotiations. Now here was Lord Darnley, in line to the English throne, and Catholic as well. The Scottish queen, while eager to become queen of Spain, was also eager to strengthen her claim to the English throne. Darnley seemed to her the perfect husband.

Mary Seton had no trouble ignoring Darnley's snubs, but Mary Fleming was not one to take such things lightly. When the four Marys were alone in the queen's antechamber, she said, "Do you know that when the justice clerk came to tell Darnley he would be made Earl of Ross, he drew his dagger, angry that he wasn't being given the dukedom of Albany, which he had wanted. And when he got a cold, the English ambassador was afraid to mention it to the countess of Lennox, because it would worry her. Imagine his mother worrying over his head colds."

Mary Beaton glared at her, "At least Lord Darnley is Catholic," she said.

"I plan to talk to the queen," said Mary Fleming. She doesn't know how he acts when she's not there. He acts as if he already own the palace." She imitated the way Darnley walked with his chest puffed.

"Don't say anything to the queen," Mary Livingston warned. "She and Darnley exchange tokens of love every day. She never acted this way over her first husband."

"And her first husband was King of all France!" said Mary Fleming.

"Lord Darnley writes her poetry in French," Mary Seton said. "I think he reminds her of happier days."

"Isn't that sweet," Mary Fleming said, "he writes her poetry. Who cares about poetry? She'd better come to her senses. With the Guises out of power and Catholicism crumbling all over Europe, she can't afford an error right now."

Mary Seton secretly feared that this was all a trick of the English queen's to get the queen of Scots into making a foolish marriage. After all, was it a coincidence that she had given permission for Darnley to journey to Scotland just after making her eccentric suggestion that the queen of Scotland marry her horse master?

Mary Fleming tried to warn the queen, as did her most trusted ambassadors, but the queen announced that she would marry Darnley and she would marry him with all the pomp and ceremony that Scotland could muster. The wedding, she said, would be Catholic.

Mary Seton felt that she was living a strange and

frightening dream as she rode through the streets of Glasgow in a carriage of the bridal procession. The queen rode ahead in a gilded French carriage drawn by white horses draped with embroidered cloth of gold and silver. The four Marys rode behind in an open carriage, shimmering in white satin and plum-colored velvet.

The Bishop of Ross, carrying a large jeweled cross, led the procession into the cathedral. The queen was confident as she knelt with Darnley before the altar under the glow of a thousand candles. The French musician played softly as Darnley raised his chin, took the queen's hand, and placed the gold ring on her finger.

Mary Seton stood beside Mary Livingston, watching. "We will pray for the best," Mary Livingston whispered.

Mary Seton nodded. There was nothing else to do.

The rumor had spread through Glasgow that the queen's own bastard half brother James Stuart – who the queen had made Earl of Murray – was leading the Protestants in rebellion. He claimed the Scots refused to accept a Catholic as their king, and wanted him instead.

"Let him rebel against me!" the queen had said. "Let him prove before the world that he is a rebellious traitor and he'll be shown no mercy."

Within hours of the ceremony, the Protestants *did* rebel. The queen herself rode at the head of the Catholic army, and within three days the rebels were beaten and driven south over the border into England. Queen Mary then declared them traitors and outlaws.

Within a week, the rebellion was put down. Mary Seton was at the Seton townhouse watching from a balcony as the queen rode into the city at the head of her army, with the people lining the streets and cheering more wildly then the day the retinue had arrived from France.

Shortly after the rebellion was put down, Mary Beaton came to find Mary Seton. "I was told to give you a message," she said, "even though I don't know how it can possibly interest you. My cousin Alexander has taken priestly vows. He will remain in the Roman church in Italy. You met him once, didn't you?"

"Yes, I did," Mary said, keeping her expression blank. "We talked about his career in the church."

"It is what my family always planned for him."

Only much later, after several hours passed and the initial shock wore off did it occur to her that Alexander might not have taken vows at all. Perhaps she had been told he had as a trick to make her more docile. She wouldn't put such tricks past her brother.

That very night, at a dance to celebrate the wedding, the queen, still glowing from victory over the rebels, offered Mary Livingston a manor house for a dowry so that she could marry John Semple. Mary Livingston kissed the queen's hands. "I will never forget how good you have been to me. Never."

Mary Seton watched, knowing the generous queen would do the same for her and Alexander, if only there were some way to get him back, which there didn't seem to be.

Of the four Marys, only Mary Livingston seemed untouched by all that had happened since they had left France. Mary Livingston had always been good natured and kind, and she spent that evening laughing as gaily as she had ever laughed at the court of France. Mary Beaton never recovered from her fright and she made no secret of her hatred of the rebels. Once she had adored Mary Fleming, imitating her and following her everywhere, but now they hardly spoke. Mary Fleming, too, had changed. Gone from Mary Seton's memory was the blue-eyed darling of the French court trailing in the wake of her young queen. Now she clung to Maitland who, to his credit, hadn't joined his Protestant friends in rebellion against the queen's marriage.

Mary Seton, who had loved Alexander and now may have lost him, had possibly changed the most of all. Her cool exterior used to be a mask that she could discard at will. But in recent weeks she felt that the part she played was sinking into her and becoming who she really was. She was frightened by the coldness she felt.

# INTERLUDE
## FOTHERINGAY CASTLE,

A loud clanging startled Lady Mary and Clare. Clare sat up straighter on her stool, and Mary Seton rose to her feet. The sound came again. The main gates of the castle were opening.

"Someone is coming," said Clare.

"Yes," said Mary Seton. "It could be the earls coming from the English Court. You must return to your room immediately."

Clare knew better then to argue at such a moment. She left the room, but did not go back to her rooms. She stood in the corridor, where she could listen to everything.

Once the girl was gone, Mary Seton pulled on a dressing gown and tapped lightly at the door to the queen's room. Already the queen was out of bed. Jane Kennedy, another of the queen's ladies, entered from her room, which also adjoined the queen.

"Quick," said the queen. "Get me dressed. I believe they're here with my death warrant."

Quickly Jane and Mary wrapped the queen of Scots in a plain black woolen cloak. She wore a heavy crucifix. Her hair, now completely white, was hidden under a black velvet cap embroidered with gold. She was old and bent with illness, but her face was so alive, her eyes so bright, one might think she was being set free or even returned to her throne. In her face were traces of the spirited young queen she had been.

She sat at a stool near the foot of her bed, facing the door, waiting, her head lifted high. Mary Seton stood close with her hand resting on the queen's shoulder. In contrast to the queen's smile, Mary knew her own mouth was pinched and tight.

Two of the queen's pages entered timidly. One went to light the torches.

"No," she said. "The dimness of these candles will suit the occasion. Let the moment remain cloaked in darkness."

When the firm knock came at the door, she said, "Enter!"

One of the queen's pages opened the door. Two men strode in., the Earl of Shrewsbury, who had been the queen's jailor before Paulet, and a man – obviously a nobleman from his dress – who Mary Seton didn't recognize. Their cloaks were so splendid, woven with fine wool and set with silk tassels and braiding, Mary Seton thought they had come directly from the English court. Behind them came another half dozen or so other men, obviously not as high ranking. Among them stood Clare's father, Paulet.

The man who Mary did not recognize stepped forward and extended a document bearing the gold wax of the great seal of England. The queen did not move to take the document.

"It is your death warrant," said the man. "Signed by the queen of England."

Mary Seton watched the Earl of Shrewsbury's face, and saw a deep sadness there. He was an elderly gentleman, and unfailingly polite to the Scottish queen, so unlike the much younger, and much more snide Paulet.

The queen crossed herself and said: "In the name of God, these tidings are welcome, and I bless and pray to him that the end of my bitter suffering is at hand. I could receive no better news and I thank the Almighty for his grace in allowing me to die for the honor of his name and his church, the ancient

Roman Catholic religion."

It was Clare's father, standing among the men, who said, "That is how you would have it remembered. You would love to die a noble martyr's death, but the world knows that you murdered your husband Lord Darnley to marry your lover. For twenty years you have tried to stir up rebellion against the queen of England."

The man who Mary Seton didn't recognize read from the death warrant, but Mary wasn't listening. Now she was watching Paulet. Mary knew that the queen of England, hoping to avoid signing the death warrant, had hinted to her ministers and subjects that one of them should quietly do away with the queen of Scots so as to save her the embarrassment, and to prevent the queen of Scots from being lifted to martyrdom by through her formal execution. None of the English queen's subjects had been willing to take the deed on themselves, so here they were, at this moment.

After the warrant had been read, the queen said, "Again, I thank you for such welcome news. You will do me great service in sending me from this world. I am glad to go. Despite my rank and royal blood, I have known only sorrow. Tonight I pity my cousin the queen of England, who knows she sends an innocent woman to her death. In the end we will face the same judge, and how will she answer for herself? Let her look to her own conscience as I have looked to mine."

She put her hand on her Bible and said: "I, Mary Stuart, rightful queen of Scotland, swear by all that is holy that I am innocent of the crimes of which I am accused."

One of the earls said, "That is a Catholic Bible. Your oath means nothing."

Mary Seton had the feeling everyone in the room was entirely conscious of the moment, each speaking lines they had written and rehearsed.

The queen smiled calmly. "If I swear on the book which I believe to be God's true word, will your lordship not believe me more than if I swear on a version in which I do not believe?"

Impatiently, Paulet said, "You will be led to the block at sunrise. Your servants and ladies will be permitted passports to France or Scotland, as they choose."

"I shall need more time to prepare," said the queen of Scots. "I shall need three days—"

"You will die at sunrise," said one of the men.

Mary Seton heard Jane Kennedy gasp, not just at the shock that there would be no reprieve and no time to prepare, but the shock of hearing an anointed queen so interrupted and contradicted.

With that, the men turned around and left. Once they were gone, in the moment of silence that followed, Mary heard the rustling of Clare's clothing just outside the door to her own room. Then Clare peeked inside.

"Why don't you just come in, child," said one of the queen's handmaids, "instead of spying at keyholes?"

"I wasn't spying!" Clare said tearfully, obviously ashamed.

"It's all right," Mary Seton said to the lady who had spoken. Mary Seton went to the doorway and whispered to Clare, "You shouldn't be here."

"I know. I'm sorry," Clare said. And then, "I'll miss you."

"I'm not going anywhere, not for a while." She drew in a deep breath and said, "We have a long night ahead."

"If I can do anything to help—" Clare said.

When Lady Mary leaned against the wall, shielding her eyes with her hands. Clare whispered, "I'm sorry for my father. I'm ashamed of the way he spoke."

"It's all right, child. You need to go back to bed now. She has much to do tonight. We all do."

# PART II:

# QUEEN MARY'S STORY

*And thus this simple queen each day*
*was wrapped in woe and care,*
*For they that have not craft and guile,*
*are first caught in the snare.*
*--Anonymous lampoon, Edinburgh, 1565*

# CHAPTER 3

The queen had her evening meal served in her own private supper room. The room was softly lit by wax candles set in iron holders, the heavy shutters closed tightly against the bitter winds. The narrow room was no more than eight feet across. Even with her elegant French tapestries on the walls, the room was dismal and small. It was impossible to imagine the queen of France dining in such a room. How she missed the spacious elegance of the Palace of Saint Germaine! How far she had come from those glorious days!

The evening was cold, with a wind rattling the windowpanes, but inside, with a fire blazing under the hooded fireplace, the room was warm and pleasant. Only five people dined with the queen that evening. With her was the earl Bothwell, a burly lowlands lord, and John Gordon, a younger son of the Earl of Arran. Also present was David Riccio, her Italian musician, Gordon's wife, and Mary Seton. Settled in snugly with a few trusted friends, she relaxed.

The queen had made it plain she didn't want to talk about

any of her current troubles, and Lord Darnley was her biggest problem. She had found out within weeks of their wedding what kind of man she had married. He gambled and drank and demanded that she give him the crown matrimonial, which would give him powers equal to hers. She had, of course, refused. Now he had laid the matter before Parliament, and at the next meeting, the issue of whether he should be granted the crown matrimonial would be up for vote.

Everyone knew if Parliament voted affirmative, which she doubted, she would veto the vote. She knew better than to trust Darnley with such powers. Among other things, should he be granted the crown matrimonial, and should she die, he would continue to reign as king. In truth, she didn't trust him not to have her poisoned if it would mean ruling Scotland as king.

The rebels also knew she would confiscate their lands and titles, and that would be the end of her brother, James Stuart – who she had recently styled the Earl of Murray, and the others who had risen up against her after her wedding.

At about the same time she realized the extent of her mistake in marrying Darnley, she also found out she was with child. Like everyone else, she hoped for a son and heir.

Tonight, she didn't want to talk of her troubles with Darnley. Tonight, she wanted to relax with a few people she knew she could trust. Mary Seton was, just then, listening quietly as the Earl of Bothwell told her about a wedding he had recently attended. The queen had never understood Mary Seton, who spoke so seldom and held herself aloof. She knew Mary Seton's gestures well: the way she folded her hands demurely in her lap and lifted her chin in a way that seemed like pride or stubbornness or haughtiness, but was none of these.

She never understood Mary Seton, but Mary Seton was one of the people in the world who she trusted completely. Having her here was a comfort.

After the dishes were cleared away and nothing remained on the table except the heavy pewter water goblets, she asked David Riccio, an Italian musician, to play for them. He picked up his guitar and began to sing.

Riccio's melody broke off in midstrain at the sound of footsteps on the back stairway that joined her husband Darnley's chambers to hers. Darnley stood on the threshold, swaying as if he had been drinking. His clothes were rumpled, and in place of his ornamental sword, he wore a crude Highland dagger.

"What are you doing here?" she said. "Take your drunkenness elsewhere!" This wasn't the first time he had burst in on her, drunk. Each time she calmly had her guards remove him from her chambers.

But then Ruthven, a member of the MacDonald clan who had rebelled against her after the wedding and had been exiled, appeared behind Darnley.

For a moment, the queen was too stunned to speak. She stood up. "What are you doing here?" she demanded.

"If it please your majesty," Ruthven said. "That man David Riccio must leave your inner chamber, where he has been too long."

She looked at David Riccio, who also served as her foreign secretary. Then she looked back at Ruthven. "Have you taken leave of your senses?"

"Riccio has offended your honor," Ruthven continued. "You have raised him to favor, a low-born foreigner, and you have banished your own subjects. All Scotland knows of your adulterous affair with him."

"It is true," Darnley said. "You know that it is."

"You have both gone mad," she said, turning to Bothwell. "Have someone remove them both from my chambers."

Ruthven said, "We have come to avenge your majesty's honor."

As if on cue, several more men appeared behind Ruthven.

In that moment, the queen understood she was under

attack. She tried to keep her shock and outrage under control. "If David Riccio has committed some offense," she said, "he shall appear before Parliament and explain himself!"

Just then, a hatchet slammed through the window shutters and five men came in through the window. Bothwell, one of the three men who had been at her supper table, drew his dagger and jumped to his feet, his knee knocking over the table. Goblets clattered to the floor.

More footsteps pounded up the back staircase. Two of the intruders grabbed Bothwell and forced the dagger from his hand. Before Gordon, another of the men at her table, could pull his weapon, several others jumped on him and flung him to the floor. Daggers were flashing and Ruthven had a pistol. Gordon's wife was on her feet, screaming.

Someone gave a whoop and all the intruders turned to Riccio. He clung to the queen's skirts, but was dragged to the other end of the room. The band of rebels surrounded him and fell on him with their daggers. His screams tapered off into a series of gurgling moans. The breath went out of the queen's lungs in a sickening gasp. This could not be happening. These rebels could not have stormed into her supper chamber and murdered Riccio before her eyes.

She looked up to see Ruthven swinging his pistol. When the pistol was aimed at her stomach, at her unborn child, she stepped back, startled, and fell over a chair. Bothwell took a flying leap and landed squarely on Ruthven, knocking the pistol from his hand.

She heard herself shouting for Bothwell to get away and get help. Bothwell tore himself from Ruthven and leapt to the window's ledge.

One of the candles tipped over and ignited a tapestry. Gordon's wife pounded the flames with another tapestry.

The rebels, swearing over Bothwell's escape, turned to her. The next thing she knew, her arms were pinned behind her and she was dragged from the room.

"You have all gone mad. Turn me loose!"

A hand was clamped over her mouth. She was half dragged out of the room and carried up the stairs. Someone's thumbs dug into her flesh, but she was too dazed to care. She was pushed into a small windowless room at the top of the stairs and a metal bolt slid into place, locking her in.

She was in pitch darkness. She groped her way along the wall, hoping for a cushioned chair or rug to rest on, afraid she would trip in the darkness and hurt her child. Despairing of finding any furnishing at all, she lowered herself onto the floor rushes and leaned back against the wall. She knew where she was. She was in a small room which had once been used for storage. In addition to the windowless room she was in, there was a smaller adjoining room in the back no larger than a closet.

A glimmer of light came from under the door, but not enough for her to see anything at all.

These rebels were perfectly capable of murdering her, that she knew. If they killed her, she would not be the first Scottish monarch to be murdered by her own subjects. A cold, chilling rage surged through her. "I hate them," she thought. "I hate them all."

Why had she insisted upon returning to this savage land to reclaim a crown worth so little? Why hadn't she listened to warning? She could now be in warm, sunny France on her French estates, or in her uncle's palaces. She wouldn't have met Darnley, so she wouldn't have made her foolish mistake.

At the time, returning had seemed the right decision. The king of Spain wasn't willing to enter the marriage negotiations unless she could reclaim her Scottish throne – he didn't want to have to retake it by force. So she'd thought she could return, reclaim the Scottish throne, then marry the heir to the Spanish dominions.

It could have happened, too, except that her cousin Elizabeth, queen of England, had interfered by saying that *she* wanted to marry the Spanish prince. Of course, she hadn't married him. She dilly-dallied and stalled long enough to spoil the Scottish queen's chance of marrying him.

So here she was, trapped locked in a windowless room of her own palace. If the French said the Scots were barbarians, they were right. For all that in her veins flowed her father's royal Scottish blood, she was ready to agree with the French. She felt a wave of deep sadness. If things had not gone terribly wrong, she might still be queen of France instead of caught in the middle of these warring, clannish Scots.

The only way the rebels could have entered the palace was with Darnley's help. She wasn't surprised that he had turned on her this way. He was stupid, but not too stupid to know that she planned to divorce him as soon as her child was born. He was therefore desperate. She hadn't thought he'd try something like this until after Parliament denied his request for the crown matrimonial.

She heard footsteps in the corridor. "Please," Mary Seton begged, "please let me in with her."

"No," said a man whose voice she did not recognize.

To her surprise, it was Mary Livingston who spoke next. Mary Livingston, who had been in Edinburgh with her family, must have rushed to the palace the moment she heard what had happened.

"The queen is with child!" Mary Livingston said. "Her child may be heir to all Great Britain! You cannot leave her in there alone!"

"Letting them in won't do any harm," said another man whose voice she didn't recognize. "And it will keep them quiet."

The metal bolt slid back. A blinding light filled the room, then the door slammed again. Both Mary Livingston and Mary Seton entered. Mary Seton carried a small candle.

"Are you all right?" Mary Livingston whispered, reaching out to touch her hands. "Are you hurt?"

The candle gave off just enough light to illuminate their faces. "I will have my revenge!" the queen said. "I swear it on my mother's grave. Tell me what is happening out there. Did

Bothwell get away?"

Mary Seton said, "Yes. I believe he went to Seton Castle. After they locked you in here, I ran to the stables. The stable boy was frightened out of his wits, but he managed to tell me that Bothwell came for horses. Seton Castle is the closest Catholic fortress."

"They've put up a guard around Holyrood," Mary Livingston said. "I came as soon as I heard there was trouble, but I almost couldn't get in."

"Who is here? Who has done this?"

"Your brother and all the other banished Protestants are back," Mary Seton said.

"My own brother. I trusted him, I gave him a position in my government, I gave him an earldom. Look what he has done to me! I swear by my life, they will all hang for this!"

"Sit down, please," Mary Livingston begged. "Think of your child. If you are not careful—"

"I will miscarry! This is what they intended. Why else would they have murdered Riccio in my presence?" She put her hand to her belly. "Darnley has betrayed me," she said, but oddly this didn't surprise her at all.

"He is weak and foolish," said Mary Livingston. "The rebels have twisted him to their purposes."

The queen squeezed her eyes closed as if she could shut his repulsive image from her mind. Her passionate love had turned to hatred so quickly she was stunned by it all.

"What can we do?" she said aloud.

"I guess we just have to wait," said Mary Livingston. "I'm sure Lord Seton will gather an army by morning. He'll get you out of here."

The queen opened her eyes and looked at Mary Livingston. "I don't think so. The rebels do not want me to live. My child will be heir to both England and Scotland, and they do not want a Catholic prince."

She remembered how Darnley had looked, swaying in the doorway while his associates had murdered David Riccio.

God, how she hated him.

"This latest outrage would never have succeeded without Darnley," the queen said.

"They must have appealed to his vanity and pride," said Mary Livingston.

"We have to win him back to our side," the queen said. "I have to get out of here, tonight. It is the only way to save my unborn child."

"How on earth will you get out?" asked Mary Seton.

"Darnley is the weakest link. Darnley will believe anything anyone tells him. He was foolish enough to believe whatever they told him, so he'll believe what I tell him."

"But how will you get Darnley in here?" Mary Seton asked.

The queen was on her feet, pacing, listening to the satisfying crunch of floor rushes underfoot. But then she stumbled against a cabinet.

"Please, please sit down," Mary Livingston begged, groping for her in the darkness. "You will make yourself sick!"

An idea came to the queen like a bolt of lightening. "That's it! I can fake labor pains! They will believe I will miscarry."

Neither Mary Livingston nor Mary Seton spoke. At last Mary Seton said, "But, what will that do?"

"Nothing would suit their plans more than my death," said the queen. "When they think I am miscarrying, I can ask for Darnley. He is, after all, the child's father."

"And then what?" said Mary Livingston.

"I will win him back to my side."

They were all silent for several very long moments. At last Mary Livingston said, "But do you really think it will work?"

"I know it will." He had not been her husband long, but she understood him well.

"All right," said Mary Seton. "Whenever you are ready."

The queen leaned back against a wall and closed her eyes. Darnley was a fool and he would be easy to trick, but her brother was wily and clever and she would have to be her most convincing.

"All right," she said, "I'm ready."

"We should move you into the back room," Mary Seton said. Mary Seton set her candle in a cubby-shelf which had been dug into the thickness of the wall. Then they all three scooped together a bed of floor rushes in the back room. Mary Livingston helped the queen settle herself in the bed of rushes.

Mary Seton and Mary Livingston then went to the door leading to the corridor and banged, screaming "Call a midwife! The queen has gone into labor! Call a midwife!"

Through the locked door, they heard the approaching of footsteps. Someone called, "What is going on?"

"The queen is in labor! Call a midwife!"

"Quiet yourselves," came a voice the queen recognized as James Stuart's, her half-brother.

"For pity's sake," cried Mary Livingston. "She will die!"

"Hush," James Stuart said through the locked door. "We will get a midwife."

The queen closed her eyes. So many times she had seen stage performances and had admired the actors who could conjure any emotion at will. Now that she needed to convince a midwife that she was in labor and ready to miscarry, she felt weak and frightened. Suppose the woman refused to believe her. Or worse, suppose she *did* miscarry.

Mary Seton came in and knelt beside her. "Are you up to this?"

"I don't know. I wonder who they will find for a midwife."

"Probably the most devoutly Protestant woman they can find. You'll have to be convincing."

When the queen heard the latch sliding open, Mary Livingston whispered urgently, "Groan! She must think you're in great pain!"

The queen had no trouble complying. She was seven months pregnant and had, during the past hour, witnessed the murder of one of her servants, had a pistol aimed at her stomach, was locked in her own castle by rebels, and understood that her husband had turned traitor.

So she moaned, pouring forth her distress and hatred, clutching her stomach and doubling over with imaginary labor pains. Mary Livingston and Mary Seton stood back to let the midwife into the small room. The midwife, a thin, wiry woman wearing a coarse woolen skirt set her lantern down beside her and knelt to examine the queen.

The queen felt the woman's hands on her. She squirmed and moaned as if in great pain. When the midwife looked up, her face was ashen. Protestant or not, she was evidently moved by the pitiful sight of her queen. "The queen is going to miscarry. Dear God, she will die!"

"Please," the queen begged tearfully, "I want my husband. Please send my husband to me."

"Of course, of course," the midwife said. She backed to the door, leaving her lantern behind. Through the partly opened door, they heard her tell James Stuart that the queen would surely die and wanted to see her husband at once.

"Pray for me," the queen told her ladies.

Mary Seton and Mary Livingston joined hands and closed their eyes tightly. The queen tried to pray, too, but found herself plotting instead what she would say to Darnley when he came.

A quarter of an hour later, the metal bolt slid back and the door to the corridor opened. Darnley strode inside, marched past Mary Livingston and Mary Seton, and entered the back room where the queen lay on the floor.

"Darnley," and reached for his hand.

"You have turned against me," he said. "You have humiliated me beyond endurance."

"We are, both of us, victims of the rebel plots."

"You are not even ill!"

She let out a groan, sobs shaking her body. She threw herself into her crying, stalling for time. "Oh, Darnley," she cried, "what are we going to do? How are we going to get out of this?"

"Out of what?"

"I am so frightened for you."

"For me? What are you talking about?" He tried to put scorn in his voice, but she could tell he was afraid.

"Don't you realize what they are going to do? Oh, Darnley, my brother is so clever and cunning. They know what you and I can do together, both Catholic and in line to the English throne. You know that the Catholics on the continent are gaining strength—"

"Your brother said otherwise."

"Of course he denied it all. See how clever he is? He knows that you and I together are no match for him. That is why he tried to turn us against each other. He almost tricked you into ruining your future."

"He told me you are trying to keep my rank below yours."

"You are my husband." She reached for his hand again, and this time he didn't pull back. She was making progress. "Why would I want to keep your rank below mine when together you and I can rule all Great Britain? They prevented you from having the crown matrimonial and then blamed it on me to make trouble between us."

"What about Riccio?"

"More of their lies! How cunning they are! Their plots almost succeeded."

"I had no part in Riccio's murder," he said. "I didn't know they would murder him. They told me they would question him and bring him to trial as your lover."

"See how they lie?" She moved closer to him. "Darnley, I have missed you so. You must love me still, I know you do. Have you missed me as I've missed you?"

"You have denied me the rights of a husband."

"Only because," she thought quickly, "only because they told me you have mistresses, many of the court ladies."

"It's not true!"

"I believed it," she said, her eyes filling with tears. "How it hurt me to think of you loving someone else!"

She hated him so much she had to squeeze her eyes shut to avoid looking at him. "Darnley, we have to get out of here."

"We can't. It is impossible now."

"We are in danger, Darnley. Both of us stand in the way of their plans. They want to get rid of both of us. My brother intends to rule Scotland. He always intended it. That is why he hates me so. He thinks that he, not I, should be the rightful ruler of Scotland. Because of your royal English blood, he resents you as well."

For several moments Darnley was quiet. Then he said, "How can we get out?"

"Go tell them that you will guard me personally. They believe you hate me. Say that I'm dying and you will inform them the moment I have breathed my last."

"Will they believe it?"

"They will if you can convince them! Oh, I know you can do it!" She kissed his hand. "For my sake, you have to make them believe you." She gave him the smile that never failed to draw people to her, to soften even her most avowed enemies.

The smile worked. He drew himself up to his full height. Then he strode through the antechamber and called for the door to be opened. Mary Livingston and Mary Seton came into the back room to sit with her. They all three listened as Darnley told James Stuart that he would guard her himself and would tell them the moment the breath left her body.

"You did it," Mary Seton whispered.

"Yes," she said, but she felt no triumph. "He's foolish enough to believe anything. My brother is probably glad to have him out of the way. Having him watch me die is a harmless enough occupation."

The hardest part of the hours that followed was keeping up her pretense that she was still in love with Darnley. She took care with every word and gesture, knowing that she couldn't afford an error now. She was almost free.

In the dark hours after midnight, she and Darnley slipped through his chambers to the back passages through the servant's quarters. Mary Seton and Mary Livingston stayed behind to hide their escape as long as possible.

The queen paused in the servants' hall long enough to grab a pair of worn leather gloves and a black hooded cloak. Then they were out in the cold night air.

They choose a gate with a single guard. Faced with both the queen and her king-consort ordering the guard to stand aside, he didn't dare disobey.

They raided a stable just beyond Holyrood and through the night they fled to Seton Castle. Her spirits returned as she listened to the thunder of the pounding hooves beneath her.

Her hair escaped from her hood and blew about her face, and the cloak billowed behind her in the wind. She'd beaten her half-brother once, when he'd rebelled after her wedding, and now she'd beat him again. It was, perhaps, true that their father had loved his mother, Lady Douglas and not her mother, a daughter of the house of Guise, who he had married because he needed the might of France behind him in his wars with the English. But despite Lady Douglas's claims on the king's heart, he had never legally married her. The crown of Scotland, therefore, was rightfully hers. Nobody could contest that her mother Marie of Guise had been legally married to the king of Scotland.

Whoever would have thought, during her years at the French Court, that one day she would have to fight like a warrior to defend her right to wear her father's crown?

Her spirits were high, but Darnley, riding beside her, was crumbling. All he could do was repeat, "We must hurry. If they capture us, they will murder us."

She looked away, sickened by his cowardice. All her life, from the first tourney she had witnessed at the French Court, she had admired courage and spirit. How had she saddled herself with such a weak and spineless husband? Since the death of her first husband Francis, her one wish had been to find a husband with whom she could rule her kingdom. She wanted a man by her side, and she had wanted one as beautiful as Darnley. Oh, why hadn't she seen the truth earlier? Why hadn't she listened to the warnings?

After several hours of hard riding, she pulled her horse to a stop. "I have to rest."

"No!" he said. "We have to go on! Think of what they will do if they capture us!"

"Darnley, remember my condition."

But he didn't care about her condition. He cared only about his safety. "If we lose this baby," he said, pulling her reins, "we can make another one."

She felt so disgusted she could scarcely look at him. "I will not gallop," she said. He therefore rode ahead. She watched him, thinking it wasn't possible for a man to be more despicable than this man who was her husband.

They reached Seton Castle before dawn. Already George Seton had gathered an army of over six hundred troops from his own estates. Bothwell and Gordon, immediately upon escaping, had dispatched messengers to all the loyal Catholics of the kingdom telling them what had happened. Bothwell then went to his own lands to gather his army. Seton appointed a troop of one hundred of the stoutest Seton clansmen to remain with the queen and protect her. With her guard, she was moved to Dumbarton Castle, where the royal armies had been summoned.

There was no time to furnish the living quarters at Dumbarton Castle, so she was surrounded by clammy bare stone walls and foul smelling rushes. Never before had she lived in such squalid conditions. She had only two Seton handmaids to attend her.

Within a few hours of her arrival at the castle, Mary Seton joined her, bringing their own maids, so soon she had something like a proper suite of attendants.

They waited for news, passing their time with their embroidery. On the afternoon of their second day at Dumbarton, in a quiet moment, Mary Seton said, "Will you do me a favor?"

"Of course! Anything!"

"My wedding to Norton is set for April. I believe these new troubles will make it impossible to have anything except a hurried wedding. Will you please write to my grandmother and tell her you wish to postpone my wedding until these latest troubles are over?"

"Is that what you really want?"

"Yes, it's what I really want."

So the queen wrote the letter, and Mary Seton dispatched it with the next messenger who came from the Seton estates.

The queen knew that Mary Seton wasn't eager to marry Norton. She knew there had been another man Mary Seton had asked the queen to intercede for, but with all the troubles, the queen had forgotten the details. But the queen didn't doubt that Mary Seton's position would be improved if she married Norton. And what woman, after all, didn't want to be married?

"You have had to suffer so much for my sake," said the queen.

"To tell the truth," said Mary Seton, "I prefer to have the ceremony postponed for as long as possible."

The queen felt unsettled by the idea that Mary Seton might actually wish to remain single. What woman didn't crave the prestige and position of being married? She herself was eager to divorce Darnley and find a more suitable husband.

Within three days, eight thousand loyal troops had been assembled from all over the realm, representing a truly national army. The queen and Mary Seton watched from a window in the north tower as Bothwell rode by in full armor, carrying a long steel lance. At his side was a silver sword sheathed in a jeweled scabbard. Behind him came foot soldiers in metal caps and quilted tunics, carrying pikes and axes. Mounted archers brought up the rear, each wearing a badge proclaiming his loyalty to Bothwell.

Before long the queen received the happy news that the rebels, knowing they were defeated, had disbanded. The queen entered Edinburgh at the head of a jubilant army, waving royal banners. She was carried in a litter because of her advanced pregnancy. The townspeople lined the streets to cheer for her. She smiled and waved.

She did not return to Holyrood Palace, however. The raid convinced her that the security was too lax there. Instead, she moved into the Castle of Edinburgh, a military fortress which Seton and Huntly and the others could secure and guarantee her safety.

Her private rooms were in the south-east corner with windows overlooking the town. She gave orders for her personal furnishings to be brought from Holyrood: her French and Italian tapestries, and the furniture she'd brought back from France, and the furnishings that had belonged to her mother.

Her first royal act after returning to Edinburgh was to issue an edict against the rebels banishing them. She would confiscate their lands and turn their estates over to more loyal lords. Shortly after she published the edict, her brother James Stuart sent a message saying that he had a document to show her which would change everything. Her council advised her to see the document, so she allowed him an audience.

He entered the audience chamber and bent his knee with proper humility, but he looked her straight in the face without shame. She wondered how he could face her after what had happened the night Riccio was murdered. Did he think she would forgot how he had behaved when he had coldly believed her on the verge of death? She would never forget, and she would never forgive him.

"You have something to show me?"

"This is a bond signed by all Riccio's murderers," he said. "A bond of association outlining the plot in detail. The purpose of this bond was to insure that no one of the assassins turned traitor on the others. You see here the signature of your husband, Darnley the King."

Horrified, she read the bond. Darnley had demanded that in exchange for helping to murder Riccio, he would be given the crown matrimonial. No wonder Darnley had been terrified! He had first betrayed her, and then he had betrayed his fellow conspirators. She was struck by the stupidity of his double deceit.

"The fool!" she exploded. "The idiotic fool!" She understood that Darnley posed the greatest danger of all, greater than her Protestant rebels, greater even than her half-brother.

"Yes, he's a fool," said James Stuart easily.

"Your name is not here," she said.

"I was traveling on the continent when this plot was hatched. I had no part in Riccio's murder. I am innocent, madam."

"Innocent, indeed! What then were you doing in the castle so quickly after the raid?"

"Those who raided your supper chamber are my friends, I freely admit that. They called me when the deed was done, and I came upon their request. But I had nothing to do with the murder of Riccio."

She considered this. How clever he was, managing to keep his name from the bond so that he could claim innocence.

"I warned you not to marry him, if you recall. I advised you that he would not make a good husband. I offer you similar advice now. I believe you must rid yourself of Darnley. You can divorce him after your child is born. I advise you to pardon your other subjects. Surely you wish to rule over a united Scotland when your child is born."

"I will never pardon anyone who murdered Riccio. Never. You may leave now."


James was not the only person advising her to pardon the murderers. Soon after, she received a letter from her cousin

Queen Elizabeth of England urging her to pardon those rebels who hadn't had a direct hand in Riccio's murder. "You must try to reunite Scotland," Elizabeth advised.

Some advice, the queen thought. Rumor was that the Protestant Elizabeth had been funding the Scottish rebels all along, and had even helped fund the Scottish Reformation.

Maitland's reason was most convincing: "If you want Parliament to agree to a divorce, you will have to permit the rebels to return. You won't have enough votes without them. Just remember that they hate Darnley more than you do. After all, he is the one who betrayed them."

Darnley was angry when he learned that she was considering a reconciliation with her rebellious subjects. He vaguely understood the position in which that left him. He had not only incurred her hatred and deepest contempt, but also that of the rebels. Had Darnley been intelligent enough to see it, he would have known that he didn't have a single ally in Scotland.

In early June, the queen entered her long, ceremonial confinement to await the birth of her child. Her midwife had been provided with a black velvet dress for the occasion. Her bed was hung with blue taffeta and blue velvet. She'd ordered Holland cloth to cover the baby's cradle.

Prince James was born during the last week of June. The birth of a male heir gave way to rejoicing through the entire kingdom. Bonfires were lit, people gathered in churches to thank God for sending a male heir.

One week after his birth, she stood on a balcony beside Darnley. Below were gathered most of the realm's nobles. "Here I swear before God," she said, "as I shall answer him at the great day of Judgment that this is your son and no other man's son." She could not resist adding, "He is so much your son that I fear the worst for him."

When Darnley did not publicly deny that the child was his, she knew that the prince's legitimacy was established. That done, she set about to get a divorce. The following day she called a meeting of her council. They met in Holyrood's darkly paneled council room.

"Divorce will be difficult to obtain," Maitland said. "If we are not careful, the child's legitimacy will later be contested."

"And the divorce must satisfy both Catholics and Protestants," said another of her councilors.

"I believe," said one of the Protestants, "that a divorce can be settled if the exiles are allowed to return."

"No," she said. "I cannot pardon Riccio's murderers." If she permitted such outrage, there'd be no telling what they would try next.

"But, madam," Maitland said. "Darnley is terrified that his co-conspirators will be allowed to return. He knows they would support you against him."

"I will never pardon them. We must find a way to get the divorce without their votes."

"The Pope will not approve of a divorce," said Huntly, one of her Catholic nobles. "He believes you have been too lenient with the heretics in your realm. He says the only thing you have done to further the cause of Catholicism in Great Britain is to marry Darnley."

"Of course," said Maitland, "there are other ways of getting rid of Darnley."

She stared coldly at Maitland for several long moments. "You cannot mean to murder him," she said.

"There may be grounds for legal execution. He is guilty of treason against you, and treason is punishable by death."

Execute Darnley? She hated him, but did she hate him enough to have him murdered?

She was afraid if she didn't get rid of him somehow he would continue to cause trouble against her, demanding the crown matrimonial, threatening to cast legitimacy on her son.

"We can convict him of treason," she said, "and imprison him so he can do no harm to me or my child."

"The punishment for treason is death," Bothwell said.

The queen turned away.

"Let us work the matter out among us," said Maitland. "we will find the grounds on which to try him."

The queen, still weary from her son's birth, was eager to end the meeting. She said, "Do nothing without Parliamentary approval. And do nothing against my honor."

A week later, a troop of Bothwell's men intercepted several letters written by Darnley to the Pope. Bothwell brought the letters to the queen and the privy council. "My wife the queen of Scotland," Darnley wrote, "is in league with the Protestants. With your help, I can rule over a united Catholic Great Britain."

The letters enraged her, as her councilors knew they would. She could see Darnley would never stop plotting against her. She agreed to let her councilors pardon the exiles to get enough votes in Parliament to divorce him. They struck what seemed to her to be a fair bargain: She would pardon some of the exiled rebels, those which hadn't had a direct hand in murdering Riccio, and in return, they would help her get parliamentary approval for a divorce. She no longer cared whether or not the Pope approved of the divorce. She wanted to be rid of Darnley.

Next she heard that Darnley was in Glasgow, stirring up trouble among his clansmen. "Madam," Bothwell told her, "he must not be allowed to remain in Glasgow. His father the Earl of Lennox will soon devise a plot on his behalf. The Lennox-Stuarts have been aiming at the Scottish crown for generations. This is the closest they have come to having it. They will not let it go so easily."

To induce Darnley back to Edinburgh, she again made vague promises of reconciliation. Soon after he arrived, he fell ill with the pox. She ordered quarters prepared for his convalescence in one of her houses on the outskirts of Edinburgh called Kirk 'o' Field. Afraid that if she left him alone, he'd begin plotting against her again, she visited him every night, pretending to want a reconciliation. In his illness, with his pale skin and reddened eyes, he seemed pathetic instead of merely repulsive.

One night when he was nearly recovered, she was so tired that she was tempted to remain at Kirk'o'Field for the night. Several of her ladies were with her, playing cards at the far side of the room; she thought they could stay too. She had ordered this room furnished with own tapestries, a chair covered with purple velvet, and a carved wooden table covered with green velvet. She could be comfortable here tonight. But Bothwell nudged her gently and reminded her that she had promised to stop at his cousin's wedding party.

When, much later that night, after the wedding party, she was in her private bedroom at the Castle of Edinburgh with the bed curtains drawn around her, she had trouble sleeping. Without fully voicing the thought to herself, she had half expected Darnley's enemies to take advantage of his illness. Poison was the favorite method of murder because afterward it was impossible to prove that there had been a murder at all. If Darnley died while feverish with the pox, everyone would believe he had died of his illness.

Soon after she drifted into an uneasy sleep, a clap of thunder shook the castle. The thunder rolled on like a row of cannons until it seemed as if the earth itself was opening to swallow Edinburgh. Then she knew the sound wasn't thunder. Jumping to her feet, she grabbed her robe and flew to the window. The doors opened and her ladies rushed in.

"What was that crack?" they asked one another, but nobody knew. In the streets below, citizens were running out of their homes carrying lanterns.

Ten minutes later, a page entered, breathless.

"Well?" the queen demanded. "What was that noise?"

"Madam, that was gunpowder. Kirk 'o' Field has been exploded. The house is a heap of rubble."

The queen clutched her throat. "Darnley?"

"Yes, Madam. Darnley was inside."

# CHAPTER 4

Several minutes passed before Queen Mary could make sense of the messenger's words. Kirk 'o' Field was blown up with gunpowder? Darnley was inside and now Darnley was dead? The messenger was watching her, waiting for her orders, but she couldn't think of what she should do.

Fortunately Mary Seton, standing nearby, stepped forward and told the messenger, "The court must go into mourning for the king. Order mourning dress for all the courtiers."

"Yes, Madam," the messenger said.

After he left, the queen threw herself across the bed and covered her head with her arms. One of her ladies of the antechamber came to tell her that Darnley had not been killed by the blast. He had escaped from the house and was caught and stabbed in the courtyard. A woman in the nearby house had heard him begging his assassins for mercy. The queen turned her face toward the wall. Why had her ladies come to tell her those things? Didn't they know she was already shocked and sickened by the thought of the explosion?

Her ladies were at the windows, watching whatever was happening outside. She tried to ignore them. She didn't want to know what was happening outside. But she knew she could not make these troubles go away, so at last she said, "What is happening?"

One of them said, "There are crowds in the streets, horrified citizens, clamoring for justice against the murderers of their king."

"Dear Lord," the queen whispered. "What shall I do?"

She could guess easily enough who had killed him: Maitland, Bothwell, and the other members of her privy council. Soon all of Scotland would know that the king had been murdered by the queen's highest ministers. Why hadn't they thought of a more subtle method? Whoever it was couldn't have hidden from the city's night watchmen the act of bringing into Edinburgh the amount of gunpowder necessary to blow up a house.

She had to do something, but who could she take action against, and who could she call on to help her dispense justice? Some of the most powerful lords in the realm were guilty of the crime. If she tried to avenge the murder, she would have to fight her own ministers and some of her most loyal lords. A new, frightening thought came to her. She had come close to spending the night at Kirk'o'Field. What if she, too, had been caught in the blast? Her next thought was even more terrifying: What would she tell the courts of Europe? She had to tell them something. She grabbed a pen and scribbled a series of letters saying that Darnley's murder had been a Protestant plot intended to kill her, too.

When the hazy light of morning lit the crevices of the window shutters, a continual stream of people came to her chambers, wanting to see her. But she couldn't face anyone.

"I am in strict mourning," she said.

She could keep her lords and statesmen out, but she couldn't keep her own ladies from talking. One said, "Bothwell and Maitland have offered a reward of two hundred pounds to anyone who can identify the murderers."

"But Bothwell is guilty," another answered. "Can you

imagine someone stepping forward to claim Bothwell's reward by naming him the murderer!"

"Anyone foolish enough to try would get a dagger in the ribs, not a reward of gold."

"Bothwell is ruling Edinburgh, and the Earl of Argyle is guarding the prince."

The queen listened, her head spinning. The top nobles in the country had murdered the king and were now dispensing justice. This was outrageous even for Scotland.

"James Stuart has left the country," one of her ladies said. "He always leaves at the first sign of trouble so he can't be blamed for anything."

Days passed, but still the queen did nothing. She had her meals served in the privacy of her rooms. Most of the ladies she sent away, keeping only a few who she trusted to remain quiet and not disturb her with endless chatter.

A week later, a message arrived from the queen's ambassador at the French court. Catherine de Medici, the queen's former mother-in-law, told her courtiers: "Queen Mary is well rid of the fool." But when they heard rumor that nothing was being done to bring the murderers to justice, Catherine said it was time for Queen Mary to take action. There must be at least the appearance of the murderers being brought to justice. Catherine's idea, evidently, was that a few underlings had to be sacrificed.

Queen Elizabeth wrote a stream of letters instructing the Scottish queen to dispense justice with a heavy hand. She insisted that Queen Mary must not make queens appear incompetent and foolish. When nothing happened, Elizabeth's letters became more energetic in their urge for action.

But the queen of Scots didn't know what to do.

One afternoon the queen was so morose she hadn't even noticed that many of her ladies of the antechamber had come into the room.

"Placards are appearing in the streets," one of the ladies of the presence chamber told her, "demanding justice for the king's death. The people accuse Bothwell, Maitland, Erskine, and MacDougal."

"Does Bothwell answer them?"

"He has answered them by assembling thousands of his own armed men and marching through Edinburgh threatening to wash his hands in the blood of anyone who dares accuse him."

"The typical response of a savage," said a French lady of the presence chamber.

Another said, "The Earl of Lennox has formally accused Bothwell of the murder. Lennox is stirring up a frenzy in the streets by showing the people Darnley's bleeding body and shouting: 'Your king has been murdered by the queen's ministers!'"

The queen turned to the window which faced a quiet, inner courtyard. She heard Mary Seton sending the ladies from the room, telling them the queen wanted to be alone for awhile. "When Mary Livingston comes," Mary Seton said, "let her in. Otherwise, do not disturb us."

Thank God for Mary Seton, who closed the door behind the chattering ladies. Mary Seton remained in the room, but she was so quiet that the queen forgot she was there. The queen rested her head on the window's ledge and closed her eyes. At times she awoke from a fitful dream and for a drowsy moment she was again the queen of France, back in the splendid glory of the French royal palaces.

"Francis," she said aloud.

In a moment Mary Seton was beside her, touching her shoulder. "It's all right," she said soothingly.

If only Francis were still alive, she would be queen of France and the wonderful French court would be hers. But those days were gone forever. She was no longer in a world of sunny green country sides and luxurious chateaux and palaces. She was trapped in this northern, rocky wilderness amid a chaotic nightmare.

"Why did we come back?" she asked Mary Seton.

"We believed the things we were told. We couldn't have known what would happen."

"Where did I make my first mistake? I want you to tell me." As she said the words, she knew she would have never asked such a thing of Mary Fleming, who had always been her favorite. Mary Fleming, she felt, would either lie, or, if she dared, give a sharp response. Could it be that she trusted Mary Seton more?

"I believe your only mistake," Mary Seton said, "was in trusting your brother, your ministers, and your subjects."

"Of course I trusted them." Even when people had warned her, she had refused to believe that an anointed queen had anything to fear from her own subjects. Nothing in her upbringing had prepared her for such a possibility. The hopeless despair she now felt was also new to her. Always her spirits had been high, and a restless ambition had possessed her. Had she really hoped to marry the heir to the Spanish empire? Had she really been delighted by the knowledge that if her cousin Elizabeth of England died without sons, she, Mary Queen of Scots, would be heir to the English throne?

According to the Catholics, Mary queen of Scotland and not Elizabeth Tudor was the rightful queen of England. There was even a time when the queen of Scots had imagined that the English would put her on the throne on place of her cousin Elizabeth. How ambitious she had once been! Now all she wanted was to return to a time before this hell had broken loose. What had made her think that she could tame this land and rule in peace? What made her think she could do what centuries of kings before her could not?

"Dear God," she squeezed her eyes shut. "What are they doing to me?" The door opened and she heard Mary Seton talking to Mary Livingston. She put her head down, wanting to hide her cheeks, which were now wet with tears. But what did she have to hide from these two who had known her all of her life?

Mary Livingston came to kneel beside her. "My dear Mary Livingston," she said. "You always come to me when I am in trouble."

Mary Livingston knelt before her and kissed her hands. "Of course I'm here. I'll always be here if you need me."

"Mary Fleming is at home with her family," the queen said, "but where is Mary Beaton?"

"She has fled to France. She will marry Ogilvy and live on his French estates."

"I am glad for her. She'll be happier there. She never did want to come back after the Reformation. So, are the streets any quieter?"

"No. People are saying the most terrible things."

"Tell me. Tell me what they are saying about me."

"They are saying that you knew of the plot to murder Darnley."

"Maybe I suspected he would be killed. So many people hated him. But I never thought they would explode the house over his head and leave me with no idea what to do! I told them to do nothing against my honor."

"That is true," Mary Seton said. "She did."

The queen looked at Mary Seton, feeling hurt by her matter-of-fact tone. Could there be disapproval in her voice? "Do you think I am a fool?"

"No," Mary Seton said. "I think you are beautiful and trusting. You told them to do nothing against your honor, and you believed that they wouldn't."

"What can I do now? What does your brother say?"

"George says order must be restored at once. He says that Europe is shocked, not because Darnley was murdered, but because nothing is being done about it."

"What can I do?"

"People expect a show of justice. Someone has to be executed for the crime."

The queen closed her eyes again. That might be true, but who could she execute? Bothwell's clansmen? She knew how stubborn and loyal the clans were – if she did such a thing she would incur the hatred of all the Hepburns.

She must have fallen asleep because the next thing she was aware of, Mary Livingston and Mary Seton were settling her head against the pillows and covering her with silken blankets.

She must have slept a long time, because when she woke up, she felt a renewed energy. There was something she wanted, and she wanted it immediately.

She pulled back her bed curtains. Mary Seton was sitting in the chair beside the bed. "I want to go to Stirling Castle," she said. "I want to see my son."

"I don't think it's safe for you to leave now," Mary Seton said.

"All I want is to see my son. Please find a way for me to get safely to Stirling Castle."

"All right," said Mary Seton kindly. "If that is what you want, that is what you shall have."

Later that afternoon, the queen was escorted to Stirling Castle by two hundred Seton troops. For three weeks she stayed at Stirling and she had her son with her every minute. His nurses and governesses stood by, idle, while she held her son and even dressed and washed him.

Hourly messengers brought letters from her privy council and from Bothwell, but she simply could not give the letters her full attention All she wanted to do was play with her son. Most of the letters she tossed aside, unopened. The few she read were predictable: Scotland could not be ruled by a woman. It was impossible. It would take all the strength of the mightiest nobles to bring order back to the realm. They urged her to make a show of justice so that she could marry again.

Mary Seton, who was her only attendant from the court, said, "They are all talking about who will become your next husband."

"I suppose that is natural," she said listlessly.

"Madam, I have never presumed to advise you, particularly

on matters of state. If I speak out of line, let our years of friendship be my excuse."

"You may speak your mind freely to me, of course. You have nothing to fear."

"Elizabeth of England has never married, and sometimes I think she has made the wise choice. Who can she choose without angering someone? If she chooses a Catholic, the Protestants will feel threatened. If she chooses a foreigner, the Englishmen resent him. If she elevates an Englishman above the others, she will create jealousy."

This is one subject on which the queen felt secure. "It is unnatural of my cousin Elizabeth not to marry. Every woman must marry."

"I think she *wants* to marry. Everyone says she is in love with her horse master, Robert Dudley. Because she can't marry him, the man she loves, she won't marry anyone."

The queen had never heard Mary Seton talk this way before. Now that she looked closely, she saw the deep calm in Mary Seton's face. She was talking about Elizabeth of England, and herself as well. Mary Seton couldn't marry the man she loved either, so she wouldn't marry anyone. The queen sensed that this was the closest Mary Seton had ever come to revealing her inmost thoughts.

"But I do want to marry," said the queen. "Perhaps a woman can rule alone, my cousin Elizabeth is managing. But I don't want to. I want a husband, and I want a strong one, not a weak fool like Darnley."

Mary Seton nodded and said, "I understand. But beware. In the chaos that is Scotland every man who has ever wanted to be king is hatching plots of how to marry you."

Her ministers wrote more letters, urging her to return to Edinburgh, but she didn't want to leave the peace at Stirling. Finally a message came which convinced her to go back. A dozen of the most powerful clan chiefs, including the ever faithful Seton, had signed a bond agreeing to follow Bothwell if he were to become king.

The queen showed the document to Mary Seton, who said, "Yes, it is my brother's signature. But I haven't spoken to him, and we don't know the circumstances under which he signed."

The queen knew that she had to return to Edinburgh to find out.

When Bothwell himself sent her a copy of the Act of Parliament which had acquitted him of Darnley's murder, she knew he was imagining himself as the next king. But the thought of marrying Bothwell, who wasn't even of royal blood, was repulsive. Darnley at least had been descended from Margaret Tudor, daughter of Henry VII, and of course, Francis had been king of France.

"You do not believe I should marry Bothwell," she said to Mary Seton.

"No, I do not," said Mary Seton firmly. "What on earth is everyone thinking? He's already *married!*"

"He's Protestant! He can get divorced without permission from the Pope. And he has a strong army. Perhaps he can restore order."

"Perhaps," said Mary Seton. "Or perhaps not. When has order ever been fully restored in Scotland?"

But Maitland sent her a message later that morning saying, "A remedy must be provided for the disorder which has fallen on the realm. Bothwell has the trust of the Catholics and the Protestants."

If anyone could restore order, it was Bothwell. The queen thought perhaps she had no choice but to trust him.

The queen's entourage had traveled less than two hours toward Edinburgh when they approached Almond Bridge, ten miles outside Edinburgh. Bothwell was waiting on the hill overlooking the old wooden bridge with an army of one thousand men.

He rode forward to speak to her. After contemplating

marrying him, his physical appearance came as a shock. Short and burly, his lips full and sensual, his eyes suspicious and watchful. He had nothing of Darnley's tall, slender beauty.

"Danger awaits you in Edinburgh," he told her. "For your protection, I'll escort you to Dunbar."

She believed him. After all, he'd never lied to her. And he'd been at the supper table the night Riccio was murdered, and had done all he could to protect her. But the idea of going to Dunbar, one of his military castles, frightened her. She would be entirely in his power, at his mercy. He'd always been loyal, but after all, he *was* Protestant.

"To prevent further bloodshed and strife," he said, this time his voice more gentle. "You must come with me."

He took her reins from her hands.

"I don't know what to do." Her own voice, which sounded so helpless and weak, surprised her. She thought again how far she had fallen.

"We have to return order to the kingdom," he said.

"All right," she said. "I'll go with you."

They rode toward Dunbar Castle. She felt safe beside him, surrounded by his army. They had gone about ten miles when he turned and shouted orders to several of his men. "Take word back to Edinburgh that I have abducted the queen by force."

When she started to protest, he said, "For your sake, this is the best way."

The sun was setting as Bothwell led Queen Mary into his castle. The drawbridge clanged closed behind them. A Protestant minister was there, ready to marry them. Bothwell had already managed to secure a divorce from Jean Gordon. The council wanted her to marry him, and all she wanted at that moment was to find a way to bring back peace. She had married Darnley for love, against the wishes of her nobility. If this was the man her subjects wanted as king, so be it. If her subjects wanted the ceremony to be Protestant, she'd comply with that, too.

# Destiny

In something of a daze, Mary Stuart, queen of Scotland, moved through the ceremony. She was married again, and this time at least her husband was no whining weakling like Darnley. Bothwell, who maintained perfect order in his Border lands, knew how to rule these Scots.

That night, alone with him, she had her first pangs of doubt. She submitted to him meekly. He made every effort to please her, but she was listless and beyond caring, beyond feeling. When she sank into sleep, her heart felt heavy.

The following morning, he advised her to publish a ban saying that she had married him of her own free will. "It will prevent the Catholic lords from attacking to avenge your honor. Remember, we must restore order." She agreed and signed the ban that he had drawn up.

By early afternoon, he was gone with his men to Edinburgh and she was left in an apartment of Dunbar Castle surrounded by hundreds of his clansmen. Always she had been surrounded by her ladies, friends, and personal attendants. Never in her life had she felt so utterly alone. She had married for the good of her realm, but she was utterly wretched. All her dreams of glory were gone: She'd never marry Don Carlos and become queen of all the Spanish dominions. She'd never have a greater crown than the one she wore. Perhaps she'd never again see her beloved France. She'd live out her days in this northern, rocky, barren wilderness.

Dunbar Castle was perched atop a rocky crag that overlooked the steep rugged coast and fishing village of Dunbar. Uneven rows of oak-framed thatched cottages dotted the hill, their protruding dormer windows framed with ivy. To the right was the sea, gray under the steely gray sky. Jagged crags, oddly shaped trees with twisted, tangled arms, and rock formations broke the line of the horizon. In the distance, the fog hung heavy, obscuring the trees and mountains, and in the air was the salty smell and whisper of the sea.

From a high window of the castle's main tower, she could see the fishing village. Two ships were tied to the dock, both bearing Bothwell's coat of arms, the crest of the Hepburns. The masts of the ships were bare skeletons, the rows of wooden fishing boats left idle every day, for the fishermen had joined Bothwell's troops, armed with pikes and axes. The royal flag of Scotland, bearing a red lion on a field of gold, was raised over the castle to proclaim her presence. Posted at the castle gates were guards wearing partial armor with red and gold breastplates. There were men in the watch tower, and soldiers on the crenellated battlements.

A small whitewashed kirk stood on a slope overlooking the village. The villagers who remained behind, mostly women, often paused as they walked along the dusty streets to peer up at the castle. She gripped the window's iron grille. They could not see her, of course. Nor could they possibly know how lonely and bewildered she felt.

One of the handmaids Bothwell had assigned to her knocked timidly on the doorframe and said: "What can we bring your majesty?"

"A dagger is all I want," she answered. "A dagger for my own heart."

She sat by herself for the remainder of the afternoon. When the sun began to set, a knock came at the door. One of the women said, "Madam, Lord Seton has come."

George Seton. She sat up and brushed the tears from her face. "Send him in please." Her mother had told her and it was true, she could always count on the friendship and support of the Seton family.

George Seton entered wearing partial armor. He tucked his helmet under his arm and set his gloves on the table that stood by the door.

"What is happening?" she asked.

"Madam, there is more trouble in Edinburgh. The Protestant lords are gathering an army to free you from Bothwell."

"Free me? They wanted me to marry him. They signed a bond of loyalty to Bothwell. Besides, he is Protestant. We were married in a Protestant ceremony."

"We'll put this rebellion down as we did the last one. The rebels are telling the people that you and Bothwell were lovers before Darnley's death and that you and Bothwell together plotted Darnley's murder so that you could marry."

"Surely nobody believes that!"

"Most people no longer know what to believe. My army has already joined Bothwell's. Huntly is bringing his men down from the Highlands."

She sighed, wondering why she had put any faith into a bond of allegiance signed by Scottish noblemen. What good was a bond of allegiance, a mere piece of parchment? The king was murdered and she had married one of the men accused of murdering him. Was anyone even interested in trying to untangle the events that had led to this calamity? Did anyone care that she had been outsmarted, tricked, led into a trap?

The following day, Mary Seton joined her at Dunbar. "You always come to me," the queen said.

"Of course. I will always be here when you need me."

They passed their time embroidering, sitting together near the hooded fireplace in a sunny room of the north tower. The queen found it odd to be alone with Mary Seton. She had never chosen Mary Seton as her favorite, having preferred Mary Fleming's vivacity or Mary Livingston's quick smile. Perhaps it was her mood of despair after all the troubles, but now Mary Seton comforted her as she was sure nobody else would. There was a quiet strength to Mary Seton which she had never noticed before.

The Seton family boasted of being the only clan in the history of Scotland that never once betrayed the crown.

"Have you heard anything of Mary Fleming?" the queen asked her.

Mary Seton looked up from her embroidery hoop. "She and Maitland were married in Edinburgh last week."

Mary Seton spoke quietly and without emotion, giving no hint as to how she felt about this marriage. But a moment later, she added, "Mary Fleming has no shame."

"It does not mean she has betrayed me. She herself has done nothing against me. She is in love with him and has been for some time. It's easy enough to remember how foolish I was over Darnley."

"I should not speak unkindly of your cousin. I know you love her. And yet, to marry Maitland of all people. I suppose I shouldn't be surprised. She has always had a taste for trouble."

Had it been anyone else, the queen would have assumed that the speaker was trying to poison her against her favorite so that she could move up in her favor, but the queen knew this was not Mary Seton's way. Mary Seton had never vied for her favor as the others had. She was speaking too simply, too dispassionately. She was simply stating the truth as she believed it, and for this the queen couldn't fault her.

"What about you?" asked the queen. "What about your wedding? If not for these troubles, you might be married now, and an English countess. Oh, I know you don't love him and didn't want to marry him. But you'd be safe now, on an English estate, far from these troubles."

"Madam, I will never marry Norton. I have no desire to live in safety on an English estate."

"But if you don't marry, what will you do?"

"I would be quite content to live out my days at the Convent of St. Pierre. But for as long as these troubles last, there is nothing I want more than to be with you and serve you, for as long as you need me, and as long as you will have me."

This last touched the queen as nothing else had for days. "Of course I will have you."

Several times each day messengers brought reports from Edinburgh. There would be a battle, no doubt about that. With such men as Huntly, Seton, and Bothwell fighting for her, the queen had no doubt that the rebels would be beaten again.

She was therefore surprised when her most trusted ambassador, Melville, arrived to tell her that the rebels had amassed a great army, and the royal forces are far outnumbered. "The two armies are at Carberry Hill," he said, "but there has been no fighting. If there is fighting, Madam, there will be only slaughter and bloodshed. There is no chance of victory."

"What are the rebels demanding?" she asked.

"They want to free you from Bothwell, and they demand a Parliamentary inquiry into the king's death, which they say you have not provided. They say they want you to dispense justice to the king's murderers."

"Who ways this?"

"Ruthven, Lennox, Douglass, Erkine—"

"That is preposterous! *They* are the murderers!"

"They accuse Bothwell."

"They were all in it together! How can the Parliament conduct an inquiry when more than half the members of the Parliament were part of the plot?"

"Perhaps they are planning to point the finger at Bothwall, to blame him. Perhaps they have grown envious of his new power and position."

Hadn't they all signed a bond of allegiance? Either that had been a trick, or enough people were trying to stir up trouble so that everything got twisted.

"Very well," said the queen. "They shall have their Parliamentary inquiry, but I don't know what they expect it to accomplish."

Mary Seton insisted on accompanying her to Carberry Hill. Just before they were ready to leave, Mary Livingston arrived with a half dozen horsemen, declaring that she, too, would go with the queen to Carberry Hill. The queen was touched by their show of friendship. They had been through everything with her. They had been there during the height of her glory when she had married Dauphin Francis, and they were here with her now.

With a troop of twenty four riders, the queen and her party off down the muddy road that led from the castle. Had the queen been in the mood to find anything lovely about her brutal country, she would have noticed that the slanting light of the sun turned a bog of wet moss into a brilliant, emerald green. She would have breathed the scent of the earth, fresh from the recent rains, and the fragrant, springy grasses sown thickly with buttercups. She would have admired the distant white birches, broken by the harsh winds, and the prickly hedges of hawthorn and thistle. But she was in no spirit to appreciate anything about this untamed land.

Within two hours the queen and her riding party approached Carberry Hill, a desolate stretch of land not far from the village of Carberry. The royal army looked pitiful against the vast armies of the rebels. Ruthven, Douglass, Lennox, Argyle and others sat on their horses in full glory, proudly bearing the arms to which their rank entitled at them. Rows of foot soldiers, their shoulder badges proclaiming allegiance to their clan chiefs, carried crude weapons. Some carried long-bows, and a few had pistols, but most carried axes designed for farm use, not warfare.

George Seton, Huntly, and Lord Herries, those who were still loyal to her, rode forward to greet her. "I shall surrender to avoid bloodshed," she told them. "And we shall conduct an inquiry into the murder of the king."

Then, surprising everyone, she turned and rode straight into the rebel army. "How is this?" she asked Lord Erskine. "I am told this is all done to get justice against the king's murderers. I am also told that you are chief among the murderers!"

Her brother James Stuart said, "Come, Madam. We are going to Edinburgh."

Edinburgh was waiting for the queen. The streets were filled with people waving banners and shouting. The crowds had evidently been waiting for hours. She guessed easily enough that the rebels had promised to deliver her. Could it be that she had been tricked again? She paused to read the banners. On one she was depicted as a mermaid who had murdered her husband.

"A mermaid?" She stopped, unable to take another step forward. Mermaids, according to Scottish folklore, were beautiful and alluring, but affairs with them always ended in disaster. Many a hapless fisherman was led to ruin by the irresistible appeal of a mermaid. The song of the mermaid was most treacherous because anyone who heard it was trapped forever.

She didn't realize she had stopped until Lord Erskine, who held her reins, pulled her forward. The people crowded in and the horses could not pass.

Lord Douglas slid from his horse. He came to her to help her dismount. "We have to walk," he said. He reached up and pulled her from her horse with too much force.

"Take care!" she said. "I am still your sovereign."

Dimly she was aware that Mary Seton and Mary Livingston were right behind her.

The people were stamping and shouting: "Burn the whore! Burn the whore!"

Whore? She turned to Mary Seton and Mary Livingston, afraid to let anyone else see her tears. "What do they think?" she whispered.

Mary Seton touched her shoulder and said, "They believe whatever they have been told. We are almost back. Just hold on a while longer."

A few blocks from Holyrood, the rebels turned away from the Cannongate. They stopped in front of a small house that belonged to the provost of Edinburgh, who was also Maitland's brother-in-law. Just then she caught sight of Maitland, standing near the front step.

"Maitland," she said, but he looked down so he wouldn't have to meet her eyes. She couldn't let herself think about Maitland or wonder if Mary Fleming was with him.

Flanked on one side by Ruthven and on the other by her brother James Stuart, she walked into the house. Mary Seton and Mary Livingston, who had been pressing close to her, were held back at the door.

When Ruthven, who was not even of noble birth, tried to take the queen's arm to lead her up the stairs to the second floor, she pulled back with a force that threw him off balance. "You dare touch my arm! You dare!"

Several others surrounded her. "Come upstairs, Madam. We want to talk to you. We want to solve this all, right away."

Bewildered, she allowed herself to be led up the stairs into a small room, dimmed with the shutters pulled against the daylight. The room was bare except for a few stools and a low table.

"What is happening. Why are we not at Holyrood? I am your anointed sovereign. No court in Europe will stand for this outrage."

Ruthven said, "We are acting at the demand of the people of Scotland."

"Subjects are commanded by God to obey their princes."

"There are those who believe that when a sovereign errs, subjects have a right to step in."

"This is treason," she said coldly.

Erskine entered with three sheets of parchment. "Madam," he said. "You are going to abdicate your throne."

"How dare you give me orders?"

"You are going to abdicate and stand aside for those capable of ruling—"

"Who is capable of ruling? You? I saw you storm my supper room and murder one of my ministers in cold blood."

Erskine spoke next. "Scotland is in turmoil. We have had nothing but civil war and unrest ever since—"

"Ever since my half-brother and others began stirring up

trouble against me!"

The Earl of Douglass said, "If you do not sign this abdication, we will charge you, in the name of the people, with the murder of your husband the king."

"You will not get away with this!"

"Madam, listen—"

"I refuse to listen to traitors!"

"I have here three bonds," said Erskine. "One is your abdication, one names your son as heir, the other names your half-brother regent of Scotland for your son's minority. You have a choice. You may either abdicate in favor of your son, or we will try you publicly for the murder of the king your husband. Madam, you will abdicate."

"This is what my brother has intended all along. But I am the rightful queen of Scotland, and I will die the queen of Scotland. Kill me if you will, but I was born queen, and I will die queen."

The Earl of Mar, another of the Protestants, went to the door and said, "Let those two in with her. Maybe they can talk some sense into her."

The door opened and Mary Seton and Mary Livingston came in. The others left and clicked the door closed behind them. "No," she turned to face them. "I will not abdicate! They may kill me and pay the price of murdering their sovereign, but I will not abdicate!"

"They are threatening to kill you," Mary Livingston said.

"Let them. They will answer for it later!"

The queen had no fear of death. Some things were far worse, such as disgracing her name forever, putting a blight on the noble houses of Stuart and Guise, being remembered as the queen who admitted to murdering her husband when she had done no such thing.

She was on her feet, pacing. Her hair had fallen loose and lay tangled over her shoulders. She pushed it aside with the back of her hand and saw that one of her sleeves was torn. The room was stifling and the crowds outside were chanting again. She stalked to the window and jerked aside the shutters.

In a moment the crowd outside was quiet. Now, as she stood looking down at them, tears came to her eyes. She saw that they were moved to sympathy and she knew the haggard and pitiful picture she must present. Acutely aware of her disheveled appearance, she stared at the suddenly subdued crowd and they stared at her.

The door to the room opened and Douglass and Erskine came in. Douglass jerked the shutters closed and again the room was dark.

The queen lifted her chin, facing them, triumphant. They did not want her stirring pity in the crowds. The people still loved her. They were lied to and tricked by these rebels, but they still loved her.

"You will sign these documents," Douglas said. "Maybe your ambassador can do a better job than these two."

Melville came in, his face somber, his eyes sad. He knelt before her. "Madam, please listen to me," he said. "They are desperate now. They know you will never forgive them. They really will kill you if you do not sign. But an abdication under these conditions can not be binding."

That was a new thought. All Europe would be horrified when they heard of an anointed sovereign held captive by her own subjects. Surely the Spanish, or her mother-in-law in France, or Queen Elizabeth would send her aid, perhaps not from love of her, but because if sovereigns could be treated thus by their subjects, no sovereigns were safe.

"Perhaps that is true," said the queen. "Papers signed under pain of death cannot be binding."

"No court will recognize this abdication," Melville said. "You must sign these documents to save your life. The moment you are free, you can renounce your abdication."

The room was still. For several moments, nobody moved.

She turned to Mary Seton, who she felt she could trust above all others. "What shall I do?" she whispered.

"I cannot presume to advise you," said Mary Seton. "But I

believe you can triumph. I don't believe you should allow yourself to be murdered at the hands of a screaming mob."

When the queen said nothing at all, Melville rose and went to the door. As if not to upset the queen's precarious calm, he opened the door with a slow and gentle movement.

"She will abdicate," Melville said quietly to the men waiting outside.

As if in a trance, but with great care, the queen wrote her signature on each of the three documents. The last thing she remembered, before Mary Livingston and Mary Seton led her to a bed where she cried herself to sleep, was Douglass saying that in the morning she would be taken to the island castle of Lochleven.

# CHAPTER 5

Next morning, Queen Mary awoke to find herself utterly alone on a mattress in a room furnished with nothing more than a dressing table and stool. She sat up and straightened her clothing. Two of the Protestant lords, Douglas and Ruthven, knocked on her door and warned her that in twenty minutes they would be setting off. She washed her face and hands in the metal basin on the dressing table. When the men came in to fetch her, she faced them with all the dignity of a queen raised at the French court.

They led her out of the house. The streets were strangely silent and still after the chaotic horrors of the day before. The sky was a deep murky gray, the air damp and cool. Surrounded by an escort of about fifty riders – including Ruthven, one of the men who had murdered Riccio – she rode northwest for several hours.

The treachery of these men went beyond anything she'd imagined possible. They'd lied and double-crossed her so many times that her head was dizzy from it all. She looked straight ahead as she rode, her pride not allowing her to look at Ruthven. She knew that they would not get away with such lies and deceit. One of her loyal lords would rescue her, publish the truth, and that would be the end of this latest rebellion and outrage.

They rode all the way to Lochleven. At the shore, several wooden boats waited to take them to the island. She had visited the island only once, but she remembered the castle well. The rebels could not have thought of a better jail, or better jailers. The castle was owned by the Douglas clan. Lady Margaret Douglas, the mother of the queen's half-brother James, had been mistress to the queen's father, James IV, and she believed that her son should have been the one to inherit the Scottish crown. She would never, ever side with the queen against James Stuart and his allies.

A high stone wall encircled the castle and the island extended only a few yards past the wall. In a storm, the waves splashed against the castle walls. Looking across the misty waters of the wide loch, the queen knew that escape from the Douglas castle would be nearly impossible.

Once on the island, she was greeted by Lady Douglas, a tall woman with her silvery-gray hair pulled severely back from her face. "I see you have come to stay with us for awhile," she said.

The queen refused to answer. She had been so gracious to Lady Douglas, inviting her to Holyrood when she'd first returned to Scotland, including her in many of the court festivities. And this was how she was thanked.

Lady Douglas said, "Your apartments are this way," and led her away from the main square tower, where the Douglas family lived, to a round tower with windows facing the widest part of the loch. She was given two handmaids and a set of rooms which had been hurriedly prepared. The walls were hung with crude red woolens and the bed made up of coarse linen.

One of the handmaids said, "Your majesty's own things have been sent for. Your majesty will be more comfortable when they arrive."

"I will be more comfortable when I am set free," she answered.

The days passed with nothing to mark them off. She spent her hours quietly with her embroidery, taking her meals in her own rooms. For the first few days, her only companions were the two handmaids who had been assigned to her, but soon she acquired another companion who quickly became her favorite. Willie, eight years old, a foundling who served as a page in the castle.

She had long, empty hours in which to think about her realm and all that had happened. How could she understand these people who were accustomed to constant feuding between the clans? The Lennoxes had always fought the Hamiltons, the Campbells and MacDonalds were ancient enemies, and the borders had been repeatedly trampled by invading English armies. The constant bickering and fighting crushed every attempt to make the realm prosperous. Elsewhere in Europe the old feudal order had long since given way to a strong central government, but the Highlanders lived an utterly separate life. Their languages and customs had not changed since Roman times, and even the Romans had not been able to conquer them. How had she expected to rule here in peace?

She sank into a melancholy mood. She felt pressure headaches all day and feverish at night. Within a few days she felt that she had always been a prisoner on this island and always would be.

One afternoon Willie came to tell her that her half-brother James had arrived to speak with her. Impatiently she tossed aside the embroidery she had been working on. For the first time in weeks she would have some contact with the outside world. She had been told nothing of what was happening in her realm. Surely the rebels could not expect to keep her a prisoner on this island forever. She thought she would appeal to James in the name of their father. She had raised him up, after all, and had given him an earldom. Surely he must have some love for her. But when he entered, she saw in his expression the same detached coldness she had heard in his voice the night Riccio was murdered.

"And pray tell me," she said, "what is happening now in my kingdom."

"The fighting has ended. Bothwell has fled and troops are in pursuit of him. If he is captured, he will be brought back to Scotland and executed for the murder of the king."

"And who will execute him? You? The others who plotted Darnley's murder? Bothwell is my husband. He is as much the king of Scotland as Darnley ever was."

"There are grounds for declaring the marriage invalid. Perhaps he was never properly divorced from Jean Gordon. Perhaps—"

"And what do you plan to do with me?"

"I was told that you voluntarily signed your abdication."

"I signed on threat of my life, as you well know."

"You abdicated in favor of your son, and you appointed me regent for his minority," he inclined his head, "and I thank you for the honor."

"What have I done, tell me, to incur your hatred? Have you no shame or honor at all?"

"I am here to tell you that your son will soon be crowned King of Scotland and to assure you that I will rule fairly in his name."

"I want my son brought to me."

"That is impossible. The council has voted it unseemly to have the future King of Scotland raised by a mother who married his father's murderer."

"You want an infant as your king. An infant cannot order you about. All along you intended to rule Scotland. Your aim from the beginning has been to stir up trouble against me."

"Are you not pleased to see your son raised to such a rank?"

When tears came to her eyes, she turned away so he wouldn't see. She would not let him gloat over her tears the way he gloated over her humiliation.

She kept her back turned, waiting for him to leave. At last she heard his footsteps as he walked from the room. The door closed behind him with a click, leaving her alone.

Next day, Lady Douglas brought her a copy of a pamphlet which had been distributed in Edinburgh in which James had given his account of his meeting with his half-sister. "When I visited her on the Island," he wrote, "she told me she is still madly in love with Bothwell and would give up her crown for him. If she could only be with her husband Bothwell, she would be content to live as a simple damsel."

"It's a vicious lie!" the queen told Lady Douglas. "Your son has no shame!"

"There is nothing to be done about it now," said Lady Douglas. "This is what the people believe."

"Because they have been lied to!"

The queen did not want to read the rest of the pamphlet. Reading it would only stir her to deeper anger. But she had to know what lies were being circulated. So she continued reading. "My sister kissed me when she saw me," James wrote, "and pleaded with me not to refuse the regency."

"He will not get away with this," she told Lady Douglas.

"It seems that he *has* gotten away with it," she said.

Next came the news that her infant son had been crowned king of Scotland, and her half-brother named as regent.

She was glad now that she had followed the advice of Melville and Mary Seton and saved her own life. At least now, alive, she had some hope of getting free and publishing the truth.

The queen soon acquired two new companions, the granddaughters of Lady Douglas, who were about eight and ten years of age. At first they crept quietly to her chambers and knocked shyly. "Your majesty?" one the older girl softly.

The other poked her in the ribs. "Grandmamma says we're

not to call her 'your majesty' because she isn't queen of Scotland anymore."

"Hush!" said the other to her sister. To the queen, she said, "Can we come in, your majesty?"

"Of course," said the queen.

At first the girls were shy with her, but they came regularly to visit her, clearly enchanted by the notion of having the famous queen of Scots in their castle. They grew more comfortable and begged for stories about the French court and her life there, and the queen, lonely and happy for their company, obliged.

After she had been on the island for two months, she looked up to see Mary Seton standing on the threshold.

"You've come!"

"Of course," said Mary Seton. "I came as soon as I could. It took this long for my brother to convince Douglass to allow me to attend you."

"Will you stay long?"

"I'll stay as long as you are imprisoned, and as long as you want me."

Seeing Mary Seton cheered the queen up considerably. She now had someone to while away the hours with, to talk and gossip and speculate about the future, and to think of possible ways to escape.

Mary Seton had brought good news. Bothwell had fled the realm, and already the rebels were fighting among themselves. As Melville predicted, the courts of Europe had refused to recognize her abdication and were horrified that she was being held a prisoner. "My brother bid me assure you that he will find a way to free you," Mary Seton said.

When Mary Seton and the queen were alone, with their heads bent over their embroidery, they talked of plans for escape. They discussed each member of the Douglas family, trying to decide which might be brought over to their side. The guards were out of the question. Ruthven and Erskine continually visited the island and switched the guards around, threatening their lives if the queen escaped. The servants, too, were out of the question, because they, too, would be fearful of their lives should they help the queen of Scots. The only link they could possibly break would be one of the Douglas family. There were the Lady Douglas's granddaughters, Willie, and John Douglas, nineteen years old, and the youngest son of Lord and Lady Douglas.

"Willie adores you," Mary Seton whispered.

"Yes, he's my constant shadow. But I don't see how a nine year old can help us much. Perhaps if John were around more."

It wasn't long before George Seton found a way to get messages in to the queen. They learned of his plan when the new laundress took Mary Seton aside and whispered, "My name's Bess and your brother George send me!"

She removed her shoe and took out a letter. "I won't say any more," she whispered. "The letter will explain."

Mary Seton waited patiently until bedtime, when the Douglas granddaughters had returned to their own rooms. She bolted the door to the queen's chamber to be sure they wouldn't be interrupted, and with a calm but happy smile, handed the queen the letter – which she herself had not yet opened or read.

"I have a plan of escape," George wrote. "Read my instructions carefully."

George explained that he'd managed to get a loyal Catholic girl, a member of the Seton clan, exchanged for the regular laundress who crossed the loch each day. His plan was for the queen of Scots to disguise herself as the laundress and leave the island with the laundry, most of which was done in town. Mary Seton to wear the queen's clothes and position herself in the queen's chambers with her back to the door. She would pretend to be praying so that nobody would disturb her.

The day for the escape was set for the following Tuesday. The queen was exhilarated by the plan. It would take more than the waters of Lochleven to hold her captive, particularly with men such as George Seton working on her behalf.

At the appointed time, Mary Seton helped her dress in the laundress's coarse linen, while the laundress hid in the wardrobe. Mary Seton tucked her own hair into one of the queen's heart-shaped caps and knelt with her back to the door.

With a scarf covering her face and hair, the queen walked through the corridor out the castle to the shore. A rickety wooden rowboat was waiting for her. She stepped inside and settled herself on the bench beside the laundry.

The boatman picked up the oars and pushed off from the shore. She looked out over the water, watching as the distant shore grew nearer. She knew George would be waiting out of sight so as not to alarm the boatman.

"Hey there, lassie," said the boatman. "You aren't the regular laundry girl, are you?"

The queen shook her head.

"Such a pleasing shape you have. You're so tall. Let me see your face." When he reached for her veil, she pulled back and looked down.

"Shy, are you? I won't hurt you. I just want to see your face."

He caught her hands. She tried to jerk herself free, but he held tight. Holding both of her hands in one of his, he pulled the scarf from her face. In his face was shock and amazement.

"What have I here? The queen of Scotland?"

"Please sir," she said, looking around. On the shore she could see the flags of Seton's horsemen. "Look! There are my nobles! The mighty Lord Seton has come to return me to my throne. Take me to the shore."

He sat staring at her. "If I did that, my master would have me murdered."

"I am your queen. Do as I say, and I will reward you richly."

"No, the infant James is King, and James Stuart is regent.

121

Helping you would be treason against them."

She said, "If I am the queen of Scotland, which you know I am, my son James is not king. I am the queen and my word is law. If you do not take me across the loch, you are committing treason against *me*."

The boatman took a minute to digest this argument. "My master said you signed your abdication."

"I signed on threat of death. I now renounce my abdication, so I am queen and you must obey me."

"I don't know who is queen or who is king, but I know who my master is, and he gave me strict orders." He rowed back toward the castle.

"Fool!" she whispered.

She considered leaping into the loch and trying to swim, but she knew she'd never make it, even if she managed to strip down to her undergarments. The distant shore was too far.

They reached the shore, and the boatman called for Lady Douglas, who gave orders for the queen to be returned to her chambers.

Once back in her own rooms, she found Mary Seton, Willie, and the laundress waiting for her. "How did they catch you?" Willie asked.

"That idiot boatman! I'd be on the other side of the loch right now, but that cursed man wanted to flirt with me."

"Humph," said the laundress. "He never tried to flirt with me."

"Well, I wouldn't feel too badly about it. He's a fool and an idiot."

Naturally enough, the laundress was banished from the island, and the Douglas family tightened their security. From now on, nobody was permitted on the island who Lady Douglas did not personally meet and verify was a loyal member of the Douglas clan.

Now that it was no longer possible to send messages

through the laundress, the queen decided to try Willie as a message carrier. The next time Willie crossed the loch, he carried a message sewn into his hem. His task was to get the message to Lord Seton. The message was sealed and containing nothing of importance, but Willie didn't know that. He was pleased with his mission and beamed with pride when he successfully delivered the message and earned a kiss on the forehead from the queen of Scots. After that they began sending actual messages through Willie.

The news they received this way was encouraging. Popular support was turning in the queen's favor. The people were indignant that their young and beautiful queen was held captive on the island by the men who – they now suspected – had actually murdered Darnley.

Mary Livingston was allowed to come for a visit. It was she who brought the news of what had become of Bothwell. "He fled to Denmark," she told the queen, "and was promptly captured by the king of Denmark, who hoped to use him in some sort of trade. He was imprisoned in a Danish dungeon. Word is that he's gone mad."

The queen shut her eyes to block the image that came to her of Bothwell, filthy and bearded, chained in darkness in a Danish dungeon.

One day a ring, smuggled to the queen from Maitland, was engraved with a mouse gnawing through the ropes that bound the lion. Mary Seton said, "Maitland always returns to your side when your cause looks hopeful."

"Then it just proves that popular support really is returning to me," she said. "If he helps me now, I will forgive the past."

It was Willie who came up with the next plan of escape. He said he could steal the key that locked the gate surrounding the castle. To prevent escape, all the boats were kept locked inside the gates. If the queen and Willie could manage to be outside the gates with both the key and a boat, they could lock everyone inside and row to freedom.

"Are you absolutely sure there is only one key?" the queen asked.

"There is one key which Lord Douglas keeps by his side at all times. The only other key is in Edinburgh for safekeeping."

George assembled the necessary support for the queen once she was freed, which made her jailers suspicious. Their suspicion fell on John Douglas, Lord Douglas's youngest son, who seemed to have fallen in love with the queen. The queen encouraged his infatuation, implying that she might take him as her fourth husband if he helped her escape. As far as the jailers were concerned, a nineteen year old in love with the queen spelled trouble, so they sent John Douglas to Edinburgh.

After John was gone, the jailers relaxed again.

The queen and her attendants planned the escape for May Day, in two months, when there would be dressing up and celebrating in the household. The queen would disguise herself as a servant and Willie would be waiting for her at the gate with the key.

Two months gave them plenty of time to lull their jailors. The queen pretended to accept her imprisonment. Once she told Lady Douglas that if she could remain on the island where she was treated so well she'd be happy all the rest of her days. She further lulled Lady Douglas by asking about John. "Perhaps, if I marry again, I can marry him and remain here on the Island."

The ploy worked. Lady Douglas, who naturally enjoyed the idea of her youngest son marrying the queen of Scots, warmed to her captive and took to showing her small kindnesses.

The day before May Day, the younger of Margaret Douglas's granddaughters ran into the queen's chambers. "I had a terrible dream!" she told the queen. "I dreamed that a black raven came and took you away and we never saw you again!"

"That's ridiculous," said the queen. "No raven is going to

take me away." All they needed was the girl repeating this dream and alarming everyone. "Talking about this dream is bad luck. If you say it enough times, it might come true."

"That's right," said Mary Seton. "And the queen doesn't want to be carried away by a black raven."

"But if you go away," the girl said to the queen. "I'll never see you again!"

"If you don't talk about that dream, and if I ever do escape, I will take you with me."

"You will? Do you promise?"

"Of course, but I don't think I'll be able to escape for a long time."

May Day dawned with no sign of rain. The girls had set up a maypole, which they hung with streamers and wreaths of flowers. They were thrilled when the queen said she would join the dancing and celebrations. The oldest of the granddaughters would be crowned the May Queen, and the queen of Scotland would pretend to crown her.

"First, the queen must say her prayers," Mary Seton said.

The girls knew the queen began each day with her prayers, which sometimes lasted a full hour.

Mary Seton stayed with the girls as the queen went into her private room to change. She first checked to be sure nobody was in the narrow alley between her window and the main castle wall, and she climbed down the ivy. She scratched her hands, but didn't care. Once on the ground, she ran to the gate where Willie was waiting for her.

"Look, I have the key!" He held up the key.

"Good," she said. "Let's hurry."

They unlocked the gate, dragged one of the boats out, and then locked the gate behind them. Her hands were trembling as they pushed the boat into the water. They were not twenty yards from the shore when two guards rattled the gate, shouting that the queen had escaped.

"Willie," she was rowing so furiously that she could

scarcely speak. "Willie, assure me again that this is the only key."

"The only other key is in Edinburgh, I promise."

"It will take them hours to get a boat over the wall."

"I told you, Lord Douglas say that it can't be done."

When they saw Lord Seton and hundreds of his men on the opposite shore, Willie grinned. "Should we throw the key in the loch?"

"You managed to steal it," she said, handing him the key. "They honor is all yours."

She looked back at the gate and saw Lord Douglas watching them through the iron railing of the gate. He was too far away for her to see his expression, but she knew he could see Willie stand up, and with all his might, hurl the key toward the deepest part of the loch. She and Willie laughed as it disappeared into the depths of Lochleven.


Lord Seton had a horse waiting for her, which she quickly mounted and they set off. How good it felt to be riding through the hills of the lowlands, free again. She lost her cap within the first hour, and her hair blew free in the wind.

When she reached Seton Castle, she was greeted by Mary Seton's grandmother, the matriarch of the Seton clan.

"There is much to do," Lady Seton said.

"There is, indeed!" said the queen. Despite her exhaustion from the long ride, she felt exhilarated.

First thing the queen did was formally renounced her abdication and issued a series of proclamations calling for all loyal subjects to help her fight the rebels. Seton made sure her proclamations were published throughout the realm. He appointed a guard to protect her at all times, while he joined the other lords who declared their loyalty to her.

Lady Seton sent an escort to bring Mary Seton home. With the queen escaped the Douglas clan had no reason to hold her there. By the time Mary Seton returned, however, the queen had already moved to the Hamilton castle.

The queen was calling her loyal subjects to her, and indeed, so many of the clans pledged their loyalty it appeared that she would emerge victorious.

Within days the royal and rebel armies faced each other at Langside. The queen watched the battle from a hillside. The only people with her were a handful of Seton riders, Willie, and Melville, her most trusted ambassador.

The royalist army outnumbered the rebel army, but not by much. It would be a difficult battle. A blare of trumpets signaled the troops to charge forward. The trumpeters kept up a continuous fanfare as the armed horsemen charged. The queen was surprised to see the Earl of Argyle at the head of the royal soldiers. She hadn't expected him to fight on her side, but the clans were continually shifting their alliances.

When several arrows glanced from the Earl of Argyle, he lifted his lance as if to charge. Then unexpectedly he fell from his horse and writhed on the ground. When he dropped, his men gathered around him, losing interest in the on-coming army.

"Treachery," Melville declared. "It was a trick!"

But there was no way of knowing why he had fallen. He seemed to have had a fit of some kind, but maybe an arrow had struck him. With Argyle down, his clansmen, led by a masked rider, shifted to the rebel side. In the chaos that resulted, George Seton tried to take charge of the royal army, but an arrow pierced the mailing beneath his arm, and he fell from his horse, his wound gushing blood.

"Madam," Melville said, pulling his horse around, "the battle is lost. We must get away from here quickly. If they capture you, they will murder you. They will take no more chances."

She knew he was right, but she couldn't move. "Look! Dear God, they have Seton!"

"Madam, you have to get away."

He jerked her reins, which brought her back to the crisis of the moment. They turned and galloped full force southward toward Maxwell's castle. They had ridden less than an hour when Lord Herries and Maxwell, two loyal lords, surrounded by a handful of their men, caught up with them.

"You got away!" she cried.

"None too soon. The casualties were high. Over thirty men are dead from the house of Hamilton alone."

"Lord Seton?"

"He's captured."

All was certainly lost. She had to get away from Scotland as quickly as possible. Without stopping once, she and her riding party galloped sixty miles toward Maxwell's castle, down a pass through the Glenkins, over trails overgrown with brush. They rode along the west bank of the River Ken where the mossy smell of the river mixed with the heavy fog of the valley. Droplets of moisture gathered around her hairline.

By the time they reached the castle, her hands were blistered and her back ached. Never in her life had she been more acutely tired. She was a strong rider, but sixty miles in a single day was too much, even for her.

"If only we could have gone to Dumbarton," Melville said, "we'd be on our way to France now."

"But who could have expected the battle to turn as it did so quickly?" Maxwell said.

They would have to flee Scotland. The only choice was to keep moving south to Solway Firth. Herries sent a small troop of men ahead to find a boat and have it waiting at the firth.

She spent the night in the Castle Corrah, in rooms which had been hurriedly prepared. The bed linen was rough wool, and there was scarcely enough fresh water for her to wash and not a single woman to attend her, but she didn't care. She was so exhausted she fell on the bed and fell instantly asleep. For the second time in her life, she was entirely without women to attend her.

The following morning, she awakened at dawn. Breakfast was cold mutton, bread with a thick crust, and apple cider. She had no fresh clothing, so she was obliged to wear the same clothing she had been wearing the day before. She was soon ready to leave again. It occurred to her that she should have her hair shorn to prevent detection. The color of her hair was too well known. She gave the orders and soon two men were brought who shaved her head.

She and her riding party were assembling just inside the castle gates when a single horseman approached the castle.

She sent a guard to find out who approached. Her guard returned and said, "A messenger is here from Seton Castle. He has a ring he said you will recognize."

The queen looked at the ring, a thin gold band set with a row of rubies. The ring was a gift she had given to Mary Seton.

"Yes, I recognize the ring. Let the messenger in."

The messenger entered and bowed. "I learned where you had gone from Maxwell's men, who recognized me. I came from the Lady Mary Seton. She wishes to go with you to France, and she bid me find out where she can meet you. She is traveling southward now."

The queen was no longer surprised by Mary Seton's willingness to leave the safety of her family castle and join her, but she was touched, nonetheless. "Tell her I will leave from Solway Firth day after tomorrow. She can meet us there, or join us later."

Soon they were on their horses again, riding southward. More than an hour passed before anyone spoke. It was Melville who said, "The sooner we are far from the British Isles, the safer I will feel."

"Are we going to France?" asked one of the riders.

"Of course," said Melville. "Where else?"

Indeed, France was the natural destination. The queen had her French estates, and her French relatives. She was queen dowager of France, so she could always claim a position in the French court. Besides, France was staunchly Catholic.

They rode on. Her gown was covered with dust and torn at the sleeves. Here she was, fleeing her realm with nothing but the rags on her back, running to the Palace of Saint Germaine where she had once ruled as queen but would now throw herself on the mercy of her former mother-in-law.

Had the French offered her aid against her rebels in the first place, none of this would have happened. Had her Guise relatives any of their former power, none of this would have happened. How could she now run, as a beggar to France, where she had once ruled as queen?

On the other hand, there was England. She may have nothing but the clothes she stood up in, but in her veins flowed the royal blood of the Tudors. She was heir to Elizabeth's throne, if not the rightful owner of it. Surely Elizabeth would receive her and offer her the due recognition as her heiress. She was mere queen dowager of France, but she was the future queen of England.

After crossing the Dee River, Herries' men destroyed the ancient wooden bridge to slow pursuit. When, on the other side of the river, they stopped for water, she told Melville, "I don't want to go to France. I want to go to England."

"England! Your majesty can't be serious."

"But I am. England is just across the firth."

"But Madam, who is in England? Darnley's family? The Puritans? Queen Elizabeth?"

"Yes, Elizabeth, my cousin. Has she not promised me assistance? Seton tells me that when the rebels imprisoned me on Lochleven, she threatened to invade if I were harmed. I have always said that the differences between us could be worked out if we could meet."

"We may not have any choice," said Maxwell. "Let's see what kind of boat we can find."

They reached the port at the mouth of the Abbey Burn in the late afternoon. The queen's party would spend the night near the ancient abbey of Dundrennan. Before unpacking for the evening, they rode along the shore until they found Herries' men with a small wooden fishing boat tossing weightlessly on the waves.

"Is that the best you could do?" Herries demanded.

"We were lucky to find this boat on such short notice," said one of the men.

"This boat will never carry us all the way to France," said Melville, "never."

The queen wandered to the water's edge, hardly aware of Herries behind her, giving orders to his men to set up camp. They would stay here for the night and continue trying to find a better boat.

This part of the firth was narrow, and on a clear day, the hills of England were visible. The doleful gray mist over the water struck a melancholy chord in her.

Her melancholy continued through dinner at the abbey and a quiet evening in which she rested in an upholstered chair near a window facing the inner gardens. She was startled by the approach of horses. Everyone in the room grew still, listening. It was clear, from the sound of the hoof beats, that only one or two riders were approaching.

Melville and a handful of Herries' men went outside to greet the riders. When she heard him call out, "It's Mary Seton," she jumped to her feet and went to the door to greet her. Mary Seton seemed to stumble from her horse. She wore a gray woolen cloak and riding hood covered with dust and bits of twigs and leaves.

The first thing Mary Seton said was, "Your hair!"

"I couldn't risk being recognized."

Tears came to Mary Seton's eyes, and she brushed them away. "How ridiculous. After everything that has happened, I cry over your hair."

"I'm not worried about my hair. We're going to England."

"England?"

"Don't try to talk me out of it. My cousin Elizabeth will surely offer me troops to help me regain my throne. If Elizabeth refuses to help me, I'll move on to the Continent. One way or another, I'll return at the head of an army and that will be the end of my rebels."

Late that night the queen lay beside Mary Seton in a large curtained bed, listening to the wind outside.

"The wind sounds like it's moaning," said the queen.

"It is," Mary Seton said. "It's talking to us, telling us not to go to England."

"I do not hear that at all," said the queen. "The wind is saying that Mary Stuart, queen of Scotland, will soon redeem herself before the eyes of the world. She will yet fulfill the glorious destiny of her birth."

# INTERLUDE
## FOTHERINGAY CASTLE,

Clare closed the door to her room, but she could still hear the pounding of hammers downstairs as the scaffold was erected. She put her head under her pillow, but still heard the hammering. She ignored the noise as long as she could. When it became too much, she thought she'd rather be downstairs where things were happening, instead of here, listening to the hammering and thinking about how, on the scaffold being built, the queen of Scotland would be executed.

She put a robe over her dressing gown and tucked her hair neatly under a cap. Once in the corridor, she heard the murmur of voices from her parent's room. Clare was sure nobody was sleeping that night.

The main hall was crowded with strangers, people already coming to watch the execution.

One man, dressed in a silk doublet with a silver cup-hiked rapier, called out to her when she poked her head from the stairway. "Girl, come here!" Several guards had put up a gold braided cord and stood by it, keeping the visitors from entering the stair towers. Clare went to where the man stood, near the gold cord.

"Will you please take a message upstairs for me?" he asked. "I have a letter for Mary Seton."

Before Clare could respond, another man said, "She's

Paulet's daughter. Don't trust her."

"Mary Seton is my friend," Clare told the gentleman in the silk doublet. "I will take her the letter."

The man studied her for a moment, as if trying to decide whether to trust her. Clare was pleased when he handed her the note and said, "Tell her I want to speak with her. Tell her Robert Norton is here."

Clare turned and ran up the stairs to the west wing, embarrassed to be bothering the queen's ladies again. At least this time she had a mission and was not just idling about.

She knocked softly on the door and said, "Lady Mary? Robert Norton is downstairs. He wants to see you and asked me to give you this note."

"Robert Norton! It's a wonder he was admitted." She opened the note, read it, and then dropped it in fireplace. "All right, let's go."

Clare led the way downstairs to the main hall. She stopped and watched as Mary Seton held her hand out to Robert Norton. Two guards stepped closely enough to hear their conversation.

"It's good to see you again, Robert," Mary Seton said.

"Mary Fleming asked me to give you this letter." When he handed her the letter, one of the guards reached out to take it.

Mary Seton said to the guard, "Really, at this late hour what harm can a letter do?" Clare was surprised to hear a lightness, even a playfulness in Mary Seton's voice. But the guard insisted on taking the letter.

When the guard left the room with the letter, Clare said: "What is he doing?"

Mary Seton said, "He's copying it to show your father. The authorities are still afraid that we might actually pull off an escape, even now."

Robert Norton smiled. "After some of the escapes you managed in Scotland, it's no wonder they're worried."

"The days for such adventures are long past, I'm afraid. If my queen were offered escape now, I don't think she would take it. Will you stay until the morning?"

"No," he said. "I refuse to watch the execution and listen to the cheers. I don't know how you will stand it."

"She must be surrounded by friends."

The guard returned and handed the letter to Mary Seton. She skimmed the letter and said, "It's just as I thought. Mary Fleming heard the end is near and has written her farewell. Thank you for coming, Robert."

"If there is anything you need—"

"No, nothing. The queen will leave me well provided for. Come along, Clare. I should be upstairs and you should be in bed."

Mary Seton actually took Clare's hand as they left the main hall. Clare, surprised by the cool feel of her fingers, so thin and long, realized it was the first time Mary Seton had ever touched her.

When they were in the stairway, Clare asked, "Do you hate the queen of England?"

She didn't answer. They were almost at the top of the stairs when Mary Seton said, "No, I don't hate her, not anymore. I did for awhile. I don't think I've ever understood her. At times she's frustrated me, and at other times I've actually admired her. Sometimes I've thought she is so wily and cunning that nobody can figure her out. Other times I've thought she's so confused that she doesn't know what she's doing. Whether she's lucky or smart, I don't know, but she has always gotten her way absolutely."

"And," said Clare, "she is having her way again. Now the queen of Scots will die."

Mary Seton stopped and looked at Clare and actually smiled. "You are wrong about one thing. Tonight the queen of England lost her battle with herself and her ministers. She did not want to sign that warrant, and for good reason."

# PART III

# QUEEN ELIZABETH'S STORY

Hark! the alarum-bell hath rung,
And the warder's voice hath treason sung;
The echoes to the falconet's roar,
Chime swiftly to the dashing oar.
Let town, and hall, and battlements gleam,
We steer by the light of the tapers' beam;
For Scotland and Mary, on with speed,
Now, now is the time, and the hour of need!
*--from "Queen Mary's Escape"*
*a traditional Scottish folksong*

# CHAPTER 6

The morning sun streamed through the wide palace windows of the chamber Queen Elizabeth used as a study. The court was then at Whitehall Palace a short distance up the Thames from London. The queen of England was sitting at a long gilded table bent over her account books. If she stood up and looked out the window, she could see the formal gardens, where painted statutes of dragons, lions, and unicorns rose above the flower banks. From the next room, where her ladies were gathered, came the scent of burning juniper wood and the sound of their chatter. Just outside the window, a carpenter was fixing a rotted gutter, his steady hammering making it difficult for her to concentrate.

Her accountants stood by watching, shuffled their feet, clearing their throats impatiently. She knew it annoyed them that she inspected the account books herself. They smiled indulgently at the thought of a mere woman troubling herself over budgets and figures. She was tired of reminding people that she had been educated alongside her brother and that she had studied mathematics since her fifth birthday.

She found what she was looking for. When she searched hard enough she could always find an error, even if it was a minor one. She stood up triumphantly, pointing to the open page. "The calculation here is wrong. Who is the featherbrain responsible for this?"

With some satisfaction she watched Sir Fortescue, a junior accountant, redden and step forward. He ran his finger down the page as he mentally added the numbers. When he reached the bottom, he cleared his throat and said: "Pardon me, your majesty. It was my error. I'll correct it." He reached for a quill.

"Never mind, I'll fix it myself," she said, taking the quill from his hand. Again he pardoned himself and then stepped back.

She scratched out his figure and rewrote it. Finished, she closed the books and dismissed her accountants. When they were gone and she was alone, she stood up and went to the window and looked outside.

She hadn't seen Cecil, her top minister all morning. She listened to the sounds of her ladies in the next room. Maybe she was imagining it, but their chatter seemed different today. Usually they laughed continually, but today their whispers sounded low and urgent. She marched out the door, through the antechamber. A few of her ladies followed her as she passed through the eight galleries leading to the council chamber.

The first thing you noticed about Queen Elizabeth, particularly when she was in an irritable mood as she was today, was the animation of her face, so full of passions and emotions. Her face, although not beautiful, was captivating and intelligent. She had pale gray eyes and lashes so light they almost disappeared, giving her a surprised, startled look. She was highly strung, and appeared frail, almost too thin to carry the weight of her shimmering silver gown. Her hair was light reddish gold, her features thin but too sharp for beauty, her skin fashionably pale.

She tried the council chamber door and found it locked. A guard was standing nearby. "Was there news this morning from Scotland?" she asked him.

"Yes, Madam, the envoy returned."

She was tempted to knock on the door and scold her councilors for calling a meeting without telling her. She knew exactly why Cecil had called the meeting. He didn't want to burden what he called her feeble, feminine mind with the burdens of government. After eight years of working with her, would he never learn?

"Tell me when the meeting is over," she said to the guard.

All she could do now was speculate on the latest calamity north of the border.

She hadn't wanted to help the Scottish Protestants during the Reformation, and she hadn't wanted to ally herself with James Stuart and Maitland, but she'd had no choice. When she had become queen of England, the Guises had controlled both Scotland and France and threatened to invade England in the name of Catholicism to put their niece Mary Stuart on the English throne. To stall for time and keep the Guises busy fighting the Scottish Protestants, she had agreed to fund James Stuart and his Protestant rebellion. Her ploy had worked. The Protestant rebellions kept the Guises busy so they had no time to think of invading England.

The last thing Cecil and his Protestant allies wanted was the Catholic Mary Stuart one day becoming their queen, so they were thrilled with James Stuart's victory and the Scottish queen's imprisonment on Lochleven, but Elizabeth had been disturbed.

Now Mary Stuart was fleeing her realm, running for her life, and there was no telling what she would do next. She was probably on her way to Spain – England's chief enemy – or worse, one of the Guise palaces, and would return to the British Isles at the head of a Catholic army, a possibility which terrified Elizabeth.

A knock came at the door. It was the guard telling her that the meeting was over.

"Now call Cecil to me."

"Yes, Madam."

When she heard Cecil approach, she began angrily pacing the damascene carpet in a show of anger. She knew exactly how to handle Cecil, and she considered displays of theatrics part of her role as queen. When he entered, she whirled to him and said, "The envoy from Scotland returned. Without telling me, you called a meeting of the council."

"Madam, how did you—?"

"How did I know?' She assumed her haughtiest expression. "Do you think I don't know what goes on in my own palace?"

"Madam, the situation is desperate. The Scottish queen never received your message—"

"She's gone to Spain," Elizabeth said, feeling weak at the thought.

"No, Madam, she has come here."

"*Here*? She has come to *England*?"

"She arrived in Workington this morning. She and her party are at the governor's house. Had she waited another day, she could have come with promises of English assistance." His expression was grave and thoughtful even when his tone was ironic. "Luck does seem to work against the sovereign lady of Scotland."

"Luck works against her," said Elizabeth, "as well as most of her subjects. And most of mine, too."

"Can a Protestant queen ever trust a Catholic with a claim to her throne? She is in the north at this very moment, pouring out her tale of woe to anyone who will listen, and you can believe she has a willing audience among the northerners, many of whom, I don't have to tell you, are still Catholic at heart. In the words of the governor, she has an 'alluring grace, a pretty Scottish accent, and a searching wit clouded with mildness,' and she has stolen the hearts of northern England."

She knew Cecil was manipulating her, playing on all her fears, but she still felt a cold panic take hold of her. "I must bring her to court at once," Elizabeth said. "She cannot be left up there were she can stir up trouble among the northern Catholics."

She could see Cecil was choosing his words carefully. "To receive her would be tantamount to recognizing her as your heiress. I remind you of your own words: 'The rising sun is always brighter than the setting sun.' Already she is holding court among your Catholic subjects. Do you want her here, at court, as your heiress?"

Cecil knew she didn't want to live in the shadow of her heir. One of her most poignant memories was when her sister was queen and everyone dissatisfied with her rule had plotted against her in Elizabeth's name.

"We can't bring her to court," Elizabeth said, "we can't leave her in the north, and we can't let her move on to the Continent. I assume you have a solution."

"The council discussed the matter at some length." Again she could see that he was choosing his words with care. "Time will work in our favor, so we suggest an inquiry to untangle the recent events in Scotland."

"She is an anointed queen and will never submit to a trial."

"It will not be a trial, it will be an informal conference. The queen of Scots will not be questioned. The rebels will be called to account for their actions."

She knew there was more to Cecil's plan than he was telling her. "When did you last communicate with James Stuart?" she asked.

He looked surprised at her question. "This morning."

"Does he know of your idea of a conference?"

"Yes, Madam. He suggested it."

That told Elizabeth everything. "And why, pray tell, would he agree to put himself on trial?"

Cecil's expression softened and a smile came into his eyes when he said, "Perhaps he wishes to clear the good name of his sister."

"I rather think he wants to keep her in England while he rules Scotland. But I don't want her here. I want her back on her throne, where she belongs."

"On her throne, where she will begin planning her next marriage? Do you want her to continue negotiations with Spain? Do you want the Spanish army north of your borders? Don't forget that the Catholics consider your cousin the queen of Scots to be the rightful queen of England."

Elizabeth glared at Cecil as if the entire mess were his fault. She had been in tight corners before, but here she was, faced by the perplexing problem of having her own rival dethroned by her subjects, arriving in her realm, asking for help.

"Madam," Cecil said, "the council feels that the solution to this problem is for you to marry."

"Marry? They're wasting time thinking about my marriage, when we're facing a crisis of this magnitude?"

"If you marry and have a son, the problem of the succession would be settled and the queen of Scots would pose no danger –"

She said, "I'll marry when the time is right, and not sooner. Now tell me who is with the queen of Scots."

She heard the edge in Cecil's voice as he said, "Maxwell, Herries, Melville, a few of Herries' men, Mary Seton, and a few Seton clansmen. Oh, yes, and a boy named Willie Douglas."

Elizabeth knew all about Lord Seton and his plans for uniting the Catholics of Great Britain. This was why he was planning to marry his sister to Christopher Norton, one of the most powerful Catholics of Northern England. They were her enemies, every one of them.

"Send Francis Knollys north to meet with the queen of Scots," she said. "Have him explain the delay in bringing her to court. She is to be treated as a guest in our honorable custody."

"Yes, Madam," Cecil said, surprised. "Knollys is perfect."

She turned away. Of course Knollys was perfect. She knew what she was doing, even if Cecil insisted on believing that she had no brains at all. Knollys was a Boleyn, one of Elizabeth's mother's relatives, and therefore a devout Protestant, a man not likely to be sympathetic to Elizabeth's Catholic rival. But Knollys, fluent in French and educated at the French Court, was also a true gentleman likely to meet with the approval of the Scottish queen.

"I want a constant report of all her activities," she said. "The Duke of Norfolk, Northumberland, Norton, and all the Catholics of the north must be carefully watched."

"Yes, Madam."

"And I've heard about that boy, Willie Douglas." She smiled for the first time. "Tell Knollys to guard his keys."

Cecil returned her smile. "Yes, Madam."

Unlike Mary Stuart, who had been raised as the pampered darling of the French court, petted and adored, a queen from birth, Elizabeth Tudor had grown up knowing that she was a step away from death. Nobody ever expected her to live long enough to become queen.

Elizabeth's father Henry the Eighth divorced his first wife to marry Elizabeth's mother Anne Boleyn because his first wife had borne him only a daughter. King Henry, like everyone else, was convinced that the Tudor dynasty needed a male heir because the rule of a woman would be disastrous. When Anne Boleyn was expecting her child, all the court astrologers predicted that the child would be male. When Elizabeth was born, King Henry was furious. He had broken with the Catholic Church to marry Anne Boleyn. When the child turned out to be a girl instead of the male heir Anne promised, King Henry believed that the Catholics were right and God was punishing him for turning away from the church.

Anne's next pregnancy turned out no better. She miscarried of a male child. The king wanted to get rid of her and make way for a new queen who could bear him a son. His first wife, Catherine of Aragon, died which meant there would be no question of his next marriage's validity – if he could get rid of Anne Boleyn. So the king accused her of treason and had her beheaded. Elizabeth never forgot that her mother was sent to the block because she had not been the male heir her father wanted.

Once, when Elizabeth was twelve, she accidentally

offended her father by mentioning her mother, and she was banished from the court for over a year. When she was allowed to return, she had learned her lesson and was thereafter careful of every word she uttered. When she was fourteen, her third stepmother was beheaded, accused like Elizabeth's mother of betraying the king. Her terrible death taught Elizabeth everything about her own mother's execution which she had been too young to remember.

When Elizabeth was twenty years old and her Catholic sister was queen, her sister had imprisoned her in the Tower because the circumstances of her birth made Elizabeth a living symbol of Protestantism. Anyone dissatisfied with her sister's rule, or any Protestant who wanted the return of their religion, plotted against her sister in her name.

If Elizabeth had any choice in the matter, she would have elected to be a religious moderate. She disliked bloodshed in the name of religion. But Elizabeth had no choice in matters of religion: To accept Catholicism would mean admitting that her own birth was illegitimate.

Elizabeth's months as a prisoner in the Tower were the worst of her life. She had passed her childhood in study, but as a prisoner she wasn't permitted books or paper to pass the time. Although she wasn't officially permitted to leave her cell, even for exercise, her jailers were aware of how close she was to the throne, so they were as kind to her as they dared to be. Twice daily, she was allowed to walk on the battlements of the Bell Tower, where she was imprisoned, but even on her walks, she was forced to endure the humiliation of two guards walking in front of her and two walking behind. She welcomed the fresh air, but the battlements overlooked Tower Green, where all executions took place, a gloomy sight indeed. She scaffold was still standing and Elizabeth, like many others, believed that she would be the next to die on it.

She knew people enjoyed telling each other that she had met Robert Dudley, her horse master, when they were both imprisoned in the Tower, but in fact Elizabeth had been in love with him since she was a child of ten and he fourteen. Robert Dudley, son of the duke of Northumberland, had often been at court and even occasionally visited her at the manor of Hatfield, where she had spent much of her childhood. But he'd never paid much attention to the pale and timid younger daughter of Henry the Eighth. Back in those days, while her father and brother were still alive, nobody ever expected her to become queen because so many people stood ahead of her in the succession.

That all changed when her brother died, leaving her sister queen – and it became clear her sister would probably never conceive. Her sister was sixteen years older than she was. It became increasingly clear that all Elizabeth had to do was remain alive and one day she would be queen of England.

Robert Dudley's father was executed for leading one of the Protestant plot against Elizabeth's sister. When Elizabeth heard that Robert had been involved in the plot, she was sure that he, too, had been executed. She was therefore surprised one day, while walking on the battlements, to see Dudley being brought into the Tower.

He held himself tensely, haughtily, angrily, and she felt she could read his thoughts in his bearing: "How dare the world deal me such a blow? I am Robert Dudley, the eldest son of a mighty duke." She smiled, thinking that he was just as she remembered: Proud, confident, strikingly handsome.

He bribed the guards to allow him on the battlement when Elizabeth took her afternoon walk. Seeing her, he ignored the guards and rushed forward, kneeling and kissing her hands. "Princess Elizabeth," he whispered, "I hoped I would find you."

It was a daring thing to do because her sister had ordered Elizabeth stripped of her title of Princess.

The guards moved to separate them, but the following week, because Dudley bribed them, the guards permitted them to sit together in a secluded stone courtyard. Dudley told her that her sister was ill and wouldn't live much longer.

Her sister's militant Catholic regime had taken to burning at the stake the most outspoken of the Protestants. After each of the burnings, the Protestants chanted: "Another Protestant burned to death, God send us our Elizabeth."

When the guards turned their backs, Dudley touched her hair and whispered that he had never noticed how delicate was her skin, how angelic the reddish gold of her hair. Her cheeks warm with a blush, she turned away coyly. "You are first noticing me because I am next in line to the throne!" she teased.

"Nonsense. You were a beautiful child, and you're beautiful now."

She believed him because she wanted to believe him, and because of the passion in his eyes. Alone in her cell, with nothing to look at but gray stone walls, shivering from the damp chill of the nearby river, weary of the politics which ruled her life, she spun fantasies: She accepted Catholicism, which meant she renounced her claim to succeed her sister. As an illegitimate daughter, she would be freed from the strains of a political life and would be permitted to live a simpler, less dangerous existence. She and Robert Dudley would marry and together they would manage their modest estates. She imagined herself as his wife and she thought if any man was worth giving up a crown for, it was him.

But they were fantasies, nothing more. By far the more pleasant fantasy was being crowned queen of England. After years in the shadows, the despised younger daughter whose birth set off a revolution, she would be worshipped and obeyed.

Elizabeth survived those years of plots and intrigues only because she had learned to lie convincingly. When Elizabeth's sister died and she inherited the throne, her first task was to hold off a Catholic rebellion. Mary Queen of Scots was then married to the Dauphin. Her father-in-law the king of France styled her queen of England. For those who believed that Elizabeth's birth was illegitimate, the queen of Scots was the next claimant to the English throne.

Everyone expected Elizabeth to marry as quickly as possible, but Elizabeth had ideas of her own. She released Robert Dudley from the Tower and gave him a position at court, making him Master of the Queen's Horse. Of all the joys of being queen, having him at her beck and call was the most delicious. She owned him, she held him in her power as surely as she held the scepter.

Elizabeth expected gossip over her flirtation with Dudley, but she hadn't expected the intensity of the resulting scandal. A year after her coronation, when word had gone so far as to say that she had given herself to her "upstart horse master," her most loyal friends and councilors begged her to marry to put an end to the terrible things being said about her. They told her that before long, her subjects would withdraw their affection, then their allegiance. She would no longer be considered worthy to wear the crown, and there would be warfare between rival claimants. The bloodshed would all be on her head and God would call her to account for it.

Elizabeth understood that she could never marry Dudley. Her subjects would never accept as king one of their own elevated above them. But she continued to flirt with him and shock those around her. Elizabeth, who had never dared step out of line for fear of losing her life, was now queen and able to do what she wanted.

Her fun came to a halt when Dudley's wife was found dead at the bottom of a stair and everyone said he had murdered her to make room for the queen. She banished him from court and talked about marrying the Archduke Charles of Austria. She had no intention of marrying the Archduke, but the negotiations quieted the scandal about Dudley.

She waited three years before bringing him back to court. She had now reached the eighth year of her reign and she knew that being queen was not a free ticket to behave as she pleased. She understood she was queen because the people wanted her to be queen and she must watch her step – at least as far as her public image was concerned.

Elizabeth was in her presence chamber, a room more than a hundred feet across, listening to one of her ladies, Lettice Knollys, playing the virginals. The room had a marble floor and was hung with rich tapestries. She sat in a cushioned armchair.

A guard at the door announced Robert Dudley. He entered and bowed deeply from the waist, his cap in his hand. She hadn't seen him since receiving news of the Scottish queen's arrival.

"Greetings, my queen."

As Lettice switched to a light, happy piece, the ladies standing nearby stepped back respectfully so as not to eavesdrop on the queen's conversation with Dudley.

"Greetings," she said. "What do you say about the arrival of my Scottish cousin?"

"I say that all of England is wondering what *you* will say."

"Are you not one of my trusted councilors and advisors? Surely you must have a plan for making it impossible for the queen of Scots to cause trouble against me."

"If your majesty married and bore a son--"

"A son will not solve the immediate danger," she said.

'Oh, but it will!'

"Pray tell me how. If Queen Mary's claim to the throne is stronger than mine, as the Catholics believe, her claim would be stronger than my son's as well. We need a more immediate solution. I trust you, my clever Robin, to think of it."

"Perhaps the right husband can be found for her, a Protestant, of course, someone loyal enough to see that she causes no trouble during your majesty's lifetime."

"Those were my thoughts exactly, my dear Robin. I suggested you. Even now you could be her husband."

"As you know, she would not have me. She thought you were insulting her."

"That is only because she has never seen you."

"Her ambitions would not allow it. She wants a husband who can bring her a greater crown than the Scottish one."

"I daresay *your* ambitions also would not allow it."

"The queen of Scots can hold no charms for me," he bent to kiss her hand. "I am waiting for another."

"I know your thoughts. Why should you settle for the queen of Scotland when you might have the queen of England instead," she enjoyed teasing him. "But you have never seen my cousin. She is well known for her beauty and charm."

Dudley smiled. "That may be, but she is pure poison as well. They say she's a mermaid, a dazing but deadly lady. Do you think I want to end like Darnley? Or Bothwell? Have I not already proven that I prefer to remain with you than marry the beautiful queen of Scots?"

"Yes, you have." She enjoyed the thought of Robert Dudley, easily the handsomest man in her court, turning down her younger and more beautiful rival to remain with her. "But you still haven't advised me on what to do about her."

"You can always fall back on your time-honored policy of running everyone in circles until they are too dizzy to know where you are leading them. Have you not run me in circles for years, playing endless games with my heart?"

"I play no games with your heart," she said, not drawing her hand back even though she knew her ladies and gentlemen were watching while pretending not to. The moment was too delicious for her to want to end it, particularly when he kissed the underside of her arm where her sleeve fell away.

"Then marry me," he said. "We will have a son and your throne will be safe."

"I would marry you in a moment, if I could. If we marry, everyone will begin talking about your wife again. They'll say we plotted her death together. Remember what happened when the queen of Scots married Bothwell?"

"You torture me so, forcing me to watch as you carry on your courtships, first with Duke John, then the Archduke

Charles, then Don Carlos of Spain--"

"You know I never intended to marry any of them. I had to pretend to want the Spanish prince to prevent the queen of Scots from marrying him."

"When will you marry me?" Again his lips touched the underside of her arm.

"I cannot marry you without throwing my realm into chaos," she said.

"Nonsense. You are the absolute sovereign of England. You yourself insist on the divinity of royalty."

Elizabeth did insist on her divine rights, but she understood what her Scottish cousin didn't: she ruled by the grace of her subjects alone. "The time is not yet right."

"I will wait forever, and I will love you forever."

.

# CHAPTER 7

Not long after, Melville arrived to speak with Elizabeth on behalf of the Scottish queen. Elizabeth was on her throne, surrounded by her ladies and court, dressed elaborately in a gown set with pearls and a large starched ruff.

"Your majesty," Melville said, "from the time the queen of Scots was fifteen years old and her uncles declared her queen of England without her knowledge or consent, you two have been set against each other, made to feel suspicious of each other. My mistress the queen of Scots believes, and has always believed, that if you can meet face to face, you can work out all your differences and come to trust each other. Are you not, after all, cousins? Is she not your closest living kinswoman?"

"I agree, Sir Melville," said the queen of England. "And we will meet. Once her name has been cleared of the false charges, I will bring her to court at once."

"If the charges are false," Melville asked, "why must she be cleared of them?"

"All for the sake of appearances, which are of crucial importance to reigning monarchs. I had heard much of the famous beauty and charm of the queen of Scots. Tell me,

Melville, is she more beautiful than I am?"

Elizabeth enjoyed Melville's discomfort. Melville was not the only person who fidgeted with embarrassment at her question. Two of her own ladies ducked behind their fans. Dudley, watching her, knew she was teasing, throwing Melville off track, keeping him off balance.

"You are  the most beautiful queen of England," Melville said, "and she is the most beautiful queen of Scotland."

Elizabeth smiled, thinking he was indeed a practiced diplomat.

"And who is taller?" she asked, standing up and raising herself to full height. "Me, or the queen of Scots."

"That is not a matter of opinion, so the answer is easy to give. The queen of Scots is taller."

"Well then," said Elizabeth, "I venture to maintain that the queen of Scots is too tall, because it is said that I am neither too tall nor too short. Now, sir Melville, please return to your mistress and tell her that soon – very, very soon – I will bring her to court and shower her with all the honors due my cousin and kinswoman."

To all outward appearances, life at the English court continued as before. Twice each week the queen held a ball for the amusement of her courtiers and nobility. She met regularly with her council and ministers. She personally inspected all account books. But at the same time, there was something different in the air which she could not quite define, something like a buzz of expectation that because something out of the ordinary had happened – the anointed queen of an independent realm had landed on English shores – more extraordinary events would soon occur as well.

Two weeks later, a steward at the door announced a messenger from Knollys. Elizabeth bid the messenger enter. As he crossed the room and bowed to her, the presence chamber became deathly still and every person in the room, even those at the far end, strained to hear what the messenger would say.

"What does Knollys have to report?" she asked.

"The queen of Scots says she will never submit to a conference. She claims the English have no right to sit in judgment of her subjects. She says she is absolute sovereign of Scotland, she declares her rebels guilty, and that is that."

Elizabeth inclined her head, it was the response she expected. She never expected a conference to actually take place, but discussing the idea permitted her to stall for time while she decided what to do next. "We will send a few trusted councilors to meet with her and discuss the matter."

"I also bring you a personal plea from Knollys. He feels his task is unusually difficult. He doesn't understand how he can monitor the Scottish queen's correspondence, keep her from stirring up discontent in the north, and at the same time maintain the pretense that she is not his prisoner."

Loud enough for everyone in the room to hear, Elizabeth said, "The queen of Scots is certainly not a prisoner." Then, she stood up and walked toward the messenger until she was close enough so that, if she spoke softly enough, only he could hear her. "As to the rest," she whispered, "tell Knollys he has his orders. It is his duty to find a way to carry them out."

"Yes, Madam."

"That is all. Return to Knollys. I want a constant report of all that happens."

On the far side of the chamber, several courtiers, including Dudley, were playing cards. A group of ladies to her left were talking about the latest fashions from France. Farthingales were narrower and ruffs smaller.

She felt too agitated to remain sitting in the presence of her court. Sweeping to her feet, she marched to the door leading to her privy chamber. Turning, she said: "Send for Cecil, please," she said. "Dudley, you may come, too."

Dudley trailed behind as she marched to her privy chamber. Soon after, Cecil joined them. When the door was closed and the three of them were alone, she exploded: "She was a fool to come here, an absolute fool!"

Cecil began, "Better here than the continent—"

"Doesn't she know what it means to be the second person in the realm? Doesn't she understand the danger she poses?"

Elizabeth's father and grandfather had methodically eliminated all rivals to the throne to make the succession safe for their Tudor descendants. But now the queen of Scots – clearly believing herself immune to danger – arrived in Workington, owning nothing more than the clothes she stood up in and the Tudor blood in her veins, insisting that Elizabeth receive her at court and pay her honor.

Cecil said, "She believes that her royalty and rank as an anointed sovereign will protect her."

"My mother and stepmother were crowned queens. Did that protect them? I was the daughter of Henry the Eighth with the rank of princess, next in line to the throne. Did that protect me when my sister was queen? You know how close I came to the block!"

Cecil and Dudley exchanged glances, and she suspected they were thinking how different her position was from the queen of Scots, even though neither of them dared say it. From the time Elizabeth was three years old until the time she was twenty-five and was crowned queen of England, she lived in the shadow of shame and a step away from death. Anne Boleyn had been called a whore, a devil who had tempted the king away from the Catholic Church. She'd been called Anne Boleyn's bastard. The Scottish queen, in contrast, was crowned queen while in the cradle, married to the king of France at the age of fifteen. Nobody had ever questioned her legitimacy or her right to rule.

Seeing how Cecil and Dudley exchanged glances, she had the unsettling feeling that everyone was in conspiracy against her.

"I want to know what people are saying," she demanded. "I trust you two above everyone."

It was Dudley who said, "People are saying that at least the queen of Scots is willing to marry, as everyone knows a queen should do."

"Marry! Yes, look at her marriages, and God save me from the same blunders. She married Darnley, a weak spineless drunken fool, turning the realm into a hotbed of rebellion and sedition. Then she married Bothwell, who, if possible, was worse! How dare anyone compare my marital choices to hers and say that I'm the fool?"

Cecil said, "At least she married and bore a son. Scotland has a prince and is assured of a masculine succession."

"We have had eight years of peace and prosperity since my coronation," she said. "Prices are low, the inflation of my sister's reign is past. Trade is prospering. But Scotland, during the past years, has seen civil war, treachery, and destruction."

Cecil nodded. "We have had good fortune, Madam."

"Fortune! You attribute my success to fortune? What have I done to invite such insults?"

"Nobody doubts that you work hard, Madam."

She wanted to hit him with the fan she carried, as she had done many times in the past. But what would that accomplish? These were two of her most loyal councilors. If they were speaking this way, what must others be saying? There must be hundreds, even thousands, who would rather see Mary Queen of Scots, who had already produced an heir, on the English throne.

Well, it wasn't going to happen. She'd been in the Tower once before, and had no plans of going back.

She turned away for a moment to compose herself and then said, "I agree completely that I must marry. The moment I can do so and insure the stability of the realm, I will marry without hesitation. In the meantime, I need one of you to come up with a plan for how can we render the queen of Scots incapable of stirring up rebellion or of bringing foreign Catholic armies to the British Isles."

Cecil said gravely, "I can think of nothing better than a

conference. We must conduct an inquiry into the recent events in Scotland."

Knowing it was just a way to stall for time, and knowing it would keep her councilors happy, she said, "Very well, Cecil. You yourself will go to the queen of Scots and convince her to agree to a conference."

There. She put it back in Cecil's lap. Let him deal with the problem.

It took Cecil many months to get Mary Stuart to agree to a conference. Upon promises that after the conference she would be restored to her Scottish throne, her impatience got the better of her and, against the advice of her friends, she declared that she was putting her faith in her cousin Queen Elizabeth. Cecil organized the conference. Melville, Herries, and Maxwell represented the Scottish queen. James Stuart and Maitland represented the Scottish nobility and a panel of English lords presided. Day after day, week after week, the conference dragged on with nothing at all accomplished. Bringing all the parties together did, however, create a perfect place for plots and intrigues. The first intrigue was for Mary Stuart to marry the Duke of Norfolk, England's leading peer, who also happened to be one of the most Catholic of the northern lords.

"Whose idea was this?" Elizabeth demanded of Cecil when she heard of it. "If the Scottish queen marries Norfolk, I will be in the Tower within three months."

Cecil agreed. "I doubt he wants to marry a deposed sovereign accused of the murder of her husband merely for her charming smiles."

"It must be stopped. Without delay."

"Yes, Madam. I will see what I can do."

The next thing that happened was that the Scottish lords insisted they wanted their queen put on trial for Darnley's murder. If she wasn't tried, they threatened to return home and leave her dumped in England.

When Elizabeth's council next assembled, she turned furiously to Cecil. "This conference has accomplished nothing, and it was all your idea. What do you plan to do next?"

It was Walsingham, another of her most trusted councilors, who answered. "We must end the proceedings in a way which will justify our refusal to restore her to her throne with full power."

"The only way to do that," said Cecil, "is to let James Stuart bring his evidence against her."

"What evidence?" Elizabeth asked.

"It is quite conclusive evidence," said Cecil, "but he will not submit it unless he receives a guarantee that she will not be restored with full power. If he accuses her openly, there will be nothing to save his life if she gets the chance to avenge herself."

She was growing impatient. The same qualities which made Cecil the best statesman in Europe could also make him the most exasperating when she wanted to wring an answer out of him. "*What* evidence?"

"Letters written in her own hand to the Earl of Bothwell proving that they engaged in an adulterous affair during Darnley's lifetime."

Who was Cecil trying to fool? She knew as well as everyone that Darnley's death was part of James Stuart's plot to gain control of Scotland. "I am the one," she said, "not you, who will take the blame for any injustice committed against the queen of Scots."

"Madam," said Walsingham, "I don't know why you are so intent on protecting her. Do you suppose that if she had the chance to become queen of England, she would protect your life?"

Cecil said, "All we ask is to present the evidence. We don't have to declare her guilty of any crime, although that would be safer."

"Very well. Allow James to bring his evidence against his

half-sister."

When the letters were presented to the conference, the Scottish queen's representatives walked out in protest, claiming the letters were forgeries. Queen Mary herself announced that the conference had been a farce and that she would not stoop to answering slanderous lies.

At about this time, Elizabeth hit on an idea for restoring Mary to her throne, while at the same time, protecting her own life. Her idea was that in exchange for restoring Mary to power, her son James would be raised in England as heir to both crowns. If both Elizabeth and Mary agreed that the infant James would succeed Elizabeth on the English throne, it would become impossible for Catholics to invade England for the purpose of replacing Elizabeth on the throne with the Catholic Mary.

Elizabeth sent the details of her plan to Queen Mary, but to her surprise, the queen of Scots wasn't interested in the idea.

Elizabeth found out the reason soon enough.

Cecil brought her smuggled letters in which the queen of Scots had been corresponding with the Philip, King of Spain, complaining of the fact that she was wrongfully imprisoned and asking for him to send armies to rescue her.

Reading the letters, Elizabeth went cold with rage.

"She wants to bring foreign Catholic troops to England," she said.

Mary Queen of Scots, who seemed not to grasp the subtleties of international relations, seemed not to understand that, should Philip of Spain invade England in the name of Catholicism, his chief aim would be to remove Elizabeth from the throne and place Mary Stuart on it.

Or perhaps she did understand it. Perhaps she understood very well that England could become Catholic only upon her own death.

"Madam," Cecil said, "there's something even more

unpleasant that I must tell you. I have a strong suspicion that Dudley has something to do with the Scottish queen's Catholic intrigues."

"And what grounds do you have for such an accusation?"

"Three of his men have been to visit her in the past two weeks."

Elizabeth, always loyal to those who loved her, was tempted to speak harshly to both Cecil for daring to accuse her favorite, but Cecil was perhaps the only man in the realm who had demonstrated as much loyalty as Dudley. She thought it best to remain quiet, for now, and watch.

That evening, as her court danced, she took Dudley aside and said, "Can you guess why the Scottish queen is not eager to pursue my plan for restoring her to her throne?"

"Perhaps she doesn't want the English to raise her son."

"But her son is now being raised by her declared enemies."

He had trouble meeting her eyes. "Then I don't understand it."

She suspected that a plot was being hatched and he knew about it. But how could that be? He had risked his life to show his devotion when she was imprisoned in the Tower. She was sure he loved her. She had raised his rank and given him riches. Surely he wanted her to remain queen. What other arrangement could suit him as well?

She began dropping hints to Dudley that she knew he was involved in whatever Mary Stuart was planning. As the summer wore on, he became noticeably more nervous whenever she talked about Mary Stuart, but still he said nothing.

Near the end of the summer, he came down with a fever and took to his bed. Elizabeth visited his sickroom each day, hoping he would spill his secret. Each day she left disappointed. One afternoon, when he was nearly recovered, he sat up in bed and she sat on a chair beside him. "You know, my dear Robin," she said quietly, "I learned many lessons in my childhood. However much I might love those who betray me, I can show them no mercy."

Under the pretense of a sneeze, he covered his face, but she could see the trembling of his hands. She waited while he wrestled with himself over whether to tell her of what he knew, and she prayed he would make the right decision.

"Madam," he said, "forgive me for not telling you sooner."

"I promise to forgive you, if you tell me everything."

"I can't bear the thought that you might be in danger. It started out innocently enough, I swear it, or I would have told you immediately. When I first knew of it, no one could call it treason."

"Tell me," she said.

"The Catholics will rebel," Dudley said, "soon. I believe the Spanish army is on its way."

Elizabeth stood up. He clutched at her hand and said, "Before you go, promise me that you believe I could never have seen harm come to you."

She knew he was lying. He had courted Mary Stuart, her successor, just as he had courted her when her sister was queen. He was telling her now of the plan now because he thought it would fail.

"Only this morning did I hear the word 'rebellion,'" he said. "I told you immediately."

"But why," Elizabeth demanded, "did she make such a foolish decision? I would have restored her to her throne!"

"She no longer trusted you after the conference. She believes you led her into a trap, then humiliated her before the world by allowing what she says are forged letters presented as evidence against her."

"It doesn't excuse what she has done, stirring up rebellion in my realm."

"I know, Madam, which is why I told you the moment I knew it was dangerous. You must believe me. Please tell me you believe me."

She should denounce him as a traitor with Norfolk, as he deserved, but she couldn't bring herself to do it. After all, he did tell her about the plot. She would forgive him and keep him with her. He would still be hers. She would guard herself against him and never, never would she trust him completely, but she couldn't give him up.

"I believe you," she said, knowing it was her weakness. She could allow herself the luxury of this one weakness if she was careful never to let her weakness destroy her.

On the first Sunday in October, in the name of Mary Stuart, queen of Scots, three hundred armed horsemen stormed into Durham Cathedral declaring that they would wipe out the rampant Protestant heresy Elizabeth Tudor had brought to the realm. They made a bonfire out of the English prayer books, erected a makeshift altar, and loudly, joyously sang Mass. They then marched to Carlisle to free the queen of Scots.

Five hundred English royal guards rushed to Carlisle, arriving just before the rebels, and whisked the queen of Scots south to the secure fortress of Tutbury. Several of the Scottish queen's messengers were captured on their way to Hartlepool and her letters were brought to the English court.

"Elizabeth Tudor has illegally imprisoned me here," the queen of Scots wrote to the Spanish king, "If you will send me aid, I will be queen of England within three months and Mass will be said all over the realm."

Elizabeth stared at the letter, furious, thinking Mary Stuart was a complete fool. Mary Stuart didn't understand the temperament of the English people, but Elizabeth did. She ordered the letters published throughout the realm and the people reacted as Elizabeth knew they would. On the streets, in the taverns, on placards hung throughout London, the people proclaimed their horror of a foreign queen bringing in foreign troops to rule them.

By December the last of the rebels had been defeated and declared traitors. The Earl of Suffolk was given the duty of punishing the rebels. When Elizabeth read the list of those

Suffolk had executed, she was again filled with fury at her Scottish cousin. The northern Catholic earls of Westmorland and Northumberland had been executed, as well as Norton and his eldest son, Christopher. Elizabeth's reign had seen its first war and bloodshed. The fighting had been costly, dozens of Englishmen were dead, and Mary Stuart was the center of it all.

"Bloodshed and disaster follow her everywhere!"

"Yes, Madam," Cecil agreed. "The unpleasant truth is that when it finally comes down to a Catholic or a Protestant England, it will come down to your life or hers. She is guilty of plotting your death, for which punishment—"

"I will not consider executing her. She came to this realm, of her own free will because I promised her assistance."

"She came because she hungers for the English crown, your crown. She came before she knew of your promise of assistance."

"She came in good faith. What will the world say if I send her to her death?"

"They will say that you are protecting your life and your realm."

Elizabeth raised her hand to silence him. She couldn't execute an anointed queen. It was unprecedented, it undermined the very foundations of government.

"Madam—"

"I will not have her murdered."

Elizabeth looked back at the list of executed Catholics, wondering if there were still those with the heart to rebel against her. Surely there were still Catholics who didn't admit defeat. "With Christopher Norton dead, here will be no Seton-Norton alliance," she said to Cecil.

"There wouldn't have been anyway, Madam. The wedding was called off a few months ago."

Elizabeth looked up, curious. She knew enough about political intrigue to know that shifting marriage alliances tell the entire story.

Cecil explained, "The letters that passed between Mary Seton and her family and friends these past few months have told the entire story. Evidently Mary Seton insisted on taking religions vows."

He leafed through the papers in his satchel and handed her a copy of a letter written from Mary Seton to Mary Livingston: "I will enter a convent before I will marry a man I despise," Mary Seton wrote. "They would not permit me to marry where I wanted, so I will never marry at all."

Elizabeth was surprised by Mary Seton's tone of defiance. Could these be the words of the most devout and pious of Mary Stuart's maids of honor? No, these were the words of a woman who had fought to escape her prescribed fate. So Mary Seton had never been a part of the Catholic marriage intrigues. Knowing of the planned marriage alliances intended to unite the Catholics of Great Britain, Elizabeth had considered Mary Seton an enemy. Now, knowing she had nothing to fear from her, Elizabeth felt sorry for this Scottish girl who had been thwarted in love.

# CHAPTER 8

Elizabeth congratulated herself on the return of peace to her realm. Once it was commonly known that the queen of Scots had sought to bring foreign troops to England, the majority of her subjects believed she was justified in keeping her in "honorable custody" where she could do no harm. The Scottish queen was not free to leave, but she was provided with a household of thirty five members, including stewards, ladies, and attendants.

After Knollys pleaded to be released from his position as custodian, she appointed the Earl of Shrewsbury as the Scottish queen's guardian. He was a dignified gentleman who pleased the Scottish queen by acknowledging her rank as anointed queen and indulging whatever whims he could without endangering the realm. He let her and her ladies go out riding – always surrounded by an armed guard. She was free to write letters to anyone she choose, but of course, he monitored her correspondence.

Elizabeth imagined that the queen of Scots had accepted the situation when Cecil called an emergency meeting of her privy counsel.

When her council was assembled, it was Walsingham,

whose spies kept watch on everything which happened in the kingdom, who reported the news.

"The duke of Anjou wishes to marry the queen of Scots," he told the privy counsel.

The duke of Anjou was the youngest brother of Mary Stuart's first husband Francis. He was coming of age and looking for a wife. The Guises, looking for a way to restore Mary Stuart to power, convinced Anjou that one day Mary Stuart would wear the English crown, so he should marry her.

"Has Mary Stuart encouraged the French?" Elizabeth asked.

"Yes, Madam," said the Earl of Shrewsbury, who had been summoned to the meeting. "She says that as an anointed sovereign, she may marry who she pleases. She also says she has the right to attain her freedom any way possible, since we are holding her illegally."

"If she agrees to marry Anjou, we will be at war with the French," she said. "They'll have the excuse they need to invade and claim both the English and Scottish crowns."

"Yes, Madam," Cecil said. "Such a marriage means war."

"It must be stopped," was all she could think of to say.

From the blank faces of her councilors, she could see that they didn't have a solution.

"I see not one of you featherbrains has come up with a plan."

None of them said a word, or moved at all.

"Only one person in this room has half a brain, and that person is me. I have my own solution – unless one of you can think of a better one."

"What is your solution, Madam?" Cecil asked.

They were watching her with both curiosity and alarm. Elizabeth herself knew of only one way to stop marriages which threatened her.

"I will offer to marry Anjou myself," she said.

Cecil, a man not easily surprised, burst out, "*You* will marry Anjou?"

"He wants the queen of Scots because he wants the English throne," she explained. "Marrying me is an easier way to get it."

Several moments passed before Cecil could speak again. "Madam, the French will never believe you will follow through."

"Why not? They know I have to marry someone soon. As you never tire of telling me, England needs an heir to prevent civil war over the succession. Who could be more eligible than the duke of Anjou?"

"Madam," said Cecil, "you said you would marry Don Carlos, but changed your mind. You said you would marry the archduke Charles, but changed your mind. The French will not be eager to have you make a fool of their prince."

"We will remind them that it is time for me to marry," she said. "I cannot postpone marrying any longer."

Walsingham said, "Anjou is a mere boy."

Yes, he was fifteen years younger than Elizabeth and about a foot shorter. If she succeeded in making Europe believe she wanted to marry him, she would at the same time make herself look ridiculous. But she knew what would happen should Mary Stuart marry him, and she preferred to look ridiculous on the English throne than look dignified in the Tower.

Elizabeth smiled coyly. "Will the French not think me a worthy bride for their prince?"

The men were all silent for a moment, looking at her, astonished. She knew they were thinking it was absurd for a woman her age to act flirtatious and coquettish. The only sullen face was Dudley's, who sat in her council as the Earl of Leicester. At last Suffolk said, "May God send our queen a husband and in time a son that our posterity may be assured of a masculine secession."

"Walsingham," she said, "you speak to the French ambassador. If the French are agreeable, you will be my emissary to France."

Cecil and Walsingham exchanged hopeful glances. Cecil said, "Let us pray to God that we are able to bring about the marriage."

The meeting adjourned with a relaxed, joyful air, so unlike the earlier tension. But Dudley, who remained behind after the others had left, was glum.

"Why the long face, my dear Robin?" she teased.

"You cannot be serious about wanting to marry Anjou."

"Come now. Have you not yet caught on to the game? I must distract the French from thoughts of Mary Stuart."

"And marrying Anjou is the answer?"

"It will be difficult to actually bring about a marriage treaty. You will be surprised at how demanding the French will be when the treaty terms are discussed. They will want things the English will never grant. The negotiations will grow long and tiresome and in the end, possibly nothing will be decided. But we will have distracted the French from ideas of rescuing the queen of Scots and putting her on my throne."

"What about me? I have to watch this happen? Madam, I beg you to find alternative." From his petulant expression, she knew what he was thinking: Whenever she began marriage negotiations, he lost prestige among the courtiers and noblemen who no longer feared that he might one day be their king.

"There, there," she said, as if to a child of six years. "Cheer up, trust in God, and be a good fellow." She tapped him teasingly on the shoulder with her folded fan.

When Anjou learned that Queen Elizabeth was interested in marrying him, he lost all interest in Mary Stuart, even though the Guises tried to stir his doubts: "If you want England," the Duke of Guise told him, "the quicker way is to marry Mary Stuart and take England by force, unless you want to spend your time dilly-dallying with an old woman with graying hair who probably can't bear children." But Anjou's advisors told him that the only way to get the English crown without war was to marry Elizabeth.

Elizabeth put on a show for the French ambassador. She carried Anjou's picture and talked of her need for a man to help her rule. She kissed his portrait and scented her letters to him. She even had Dudley convinced, and she had told him it was all a farce.

Dudley retaliated by flirting with all the youngest and prettiest ladies of her court, which enraged her. One evening, what should have been a pleasant hour of lute-playing and dancing, instead turned into an evening in which she was forced to watch him flirting with Lettice Knollys. After most of her courtiers had gone to bed, when she could speak to him privately, she said, "You are behaving like a child!"

His calm surprised her. "I, too, want a son. I now hold an earldom. I have a duty to provide an heir to my domain."

She turned away, feeling her anger rise. She didn't want to admit that her anger and jealousy was as unreasonable as his.

Despite her nagging annoyance over Dudley, she enjoyed carrying on her flirtation with Anjou, basking in the compliments she received from the French ambassador. When she protested that Anjou would think her too old, the ambassador assured her that she was so youthful that nobody would guess her age a day over twenty.

Elizabeth's only worry was that Philip of Spain was too quiet. He, like Mary Stuart, would feel frustrated at the thought of a marriage alliance between France and England. Elizabeth and her council therefore expected them to enter a plot together.

"If the queen of Scots has acquired any instincts of self-preservation," Elizabeth told Cecil, "she will know enough to keep her name from being linked to whatever Philip tries next."

"To expect common sense from the queen of Scots," said Cecil, "would be to look for the sun at midnight."

Within the month Elizabeth received a private warning that a plot was afoot involving Rome, the Spanish, Mary

Stuart, and a man named Ridolfi. Walsingham had his spies find out what they could about Ridolfi, and they learned that he was a wealthy Italian banker living in London. He had recently returned from a journey through the continent which included a visit to Philip of Spain and the Pope.

When Walsingham's agents searched one of Ridolphi's servants, they found a packet of incriminating letters. It turned out that the Catholic duke of Norfolk was plotting to marry the queen of Scots and claim the English throne for her. Philip had agreed to send in ten thousand Spanish troops after Mary Stuart escaped or Elizabeth was assassinated. The Pope wrote sanctioning the plot in the name of Catholicism.

Elizabeth dispatched Cecil to Tutbury, where the queen of Scots was then in residence, to meet with her. Cecil returned three days later to report on his conference with the Queen of Scots.

He described her as composed and outwardly calm, waiting for him in the receiving room just below her private chambers. The Earl of Shrewsbury had permitted her to set up her cloth of state and she sat proudly beneath it, surrounded by her ladies and servants as if she were still a reigning queen.

When Cecil accused her of plotting Elizabeth's murder, she said, "I deny having plotted to overthrow the government or harm the queen of England in any way. I was led to believe that marriage between Norfolk and myself would meet with English approval."

When Cecil accused her of claiming the English throne, she said, "I do admit to bearing the title of England when I was a young girl and under the command of my uncle the Duke of Guise, but not since."

When he asked her about Ridolfi, she said, "I will answer no further questions until I am permitted personally to address the English Parliament. As a sovereign, I do not recognize your jurisdiction over me."

The duke of Norfolk was tried by the Parliament, and convicted on the evidence of the Scottish queen's letters. He was executed for treason, and again, Elizabeth's fury was directed against the queen of Scots. Until her arrival in England, the realm had experienced peace and prosperity. Since her arrival, there had been discord and treason. Now, another of her noblemen had been executed.

After his execution, a committee from the House of Commons petitioned Elizabeth to put the queen of Scots on trial.

"Madam," the Speaker of the House said to Elizabeth, "she has seduced the duke from his allegiance, she encouraged rebellion in the north, she conspired with Ridolfi to bring in foreign soldiers, and she has called herself queen of England during your majesty's lifetime. The sword must give her the next warning."

"Can I put to death the bird that to escape the hawk has fled to my feet for protection? Honor and conscience forbid."

These were Elizabeth's public words, but inwardly she cursed Mary Stuart for being the sole cause of all her troubles.

Six months after the rebellion, Mary Stuart asked permission for two additional people to join her household. Elizabeth, ever frugal, had no wish to see the Scottish queen's already costly household expanded any further.

The queen's first request was for a Scottish lady named Jane Kennedy to enter her service as an attendant. Walsingham checked into her background and concluded that although her family was still Catholic, they were powerless and Jane was a harmless addition to the Scottish queen's household. Jane had a good reason for wanting to serve the captive queen of Scots: she had recently been widowed and didn't want to remarry.

The second applicant to the Scottish queen's household was Alexander Beaton, nephew of the Archbishop.

Walsingham recommended that the request be denied. Alexander had grown up in the church and would have been ordained had the Reformation in Scotland not had made it impossible. "The last thing we need are any more Catholic priests in England," Walsingham said, and Elizabeth agreed. Thinking that would end the matter, she signed a letter informing Alexander Beaton that his request had been denied.

To Elizabeth's surprise, Alexander Beaton persisted in asking permission to join the Scottish queen's household, sending pleading letters to the English Council. She asked Walsingham, who had an extensive spy network, to find out what he could about Alexander Beaton.

Walsingham reported back: "He's always been out of step with his uncles, who are disturbed by his desire to join the queen of Scots. For some reason, several years ago, he was banished from the Scottish court. It seems that he was also banished from the French court when Mary Stuart married the dauphin."

"Why, then, does he want to join her household now?"

"He says his reasons are personal. He wants an audience to tell you his reasons."

"I see no reason for the archbishop's nephew to come to England," she said.

"I could not agree more. I am only surprised the archbishop would choose so obvious a spy."

After two more pleading letters from Alexander Beaton, curiosity got the better of her and she granted him an audience.

She was sitting with her ladies in her antechamber. All afternoon she had been granting audiences, and she was tired. But when her steward announced, "Alexander Beaton," she perked up, curious.

The moment he entered, she sensed she had nothing to fear from him, even if his uncle had been pope instead of archbishop. He had a broad, friendly face framed by thick, soft brown hair. Elizabeth sensed he was a little afraid even though he tried not to show it.

"You have something to say to me?" she asked.

"Yes, Madam. The Scottish queen's master of the household has recently left his post. I wish to apply for the position."

"Surely you can find a better position in Scotland, or in your uncle's French administration."

"I do not want a better position, Madam."

"Twice you were banished from the Scottish queen's court. Why do you want to return? Why does she want you back?"

She saw his astonishment and felt pleased. Did he think such trivial details were beyond the reach of her spies?

"The queen of Scots never knew of those incidents. The Duke of Guise and Lord Seton banished me without her knowledge because they knew I wanted to marry Lord Seton's sister." He paused and said, "But she was already betrothed to Christopher Norton."

Elizabeth shot him a quick glance: The Nortons and Setons had kept that betrothal secret. Had Walsingham's spies not been so good, she would never have known about it. But here was Alexander, speaking lightly of Catholic marriage plots.

"Christopher Norton is dead," she said.

"Yes, Madam. I know that."

Remembering Mary Seton's letter, she guessed the entire story: this was the man Mary Seton had wanted to marry.

"Now you wish to return to Mary Seton."

"Yes, Madam, that is my wish."

"Why didn't you return sooner?"

"Until now my Catholic kinsmen have prevented me." A hint of smile came into his eyes when he said, "But the Catholics no longer have the power they once did, as your majesty is well aware."

"Indeed," she said, allowing her expression to relax. Alexander Beaton wanted to join the queen's household because he was in love with Mary Seton and had been in love with her for years. It was that simple. All of Elizabeth's instincts, which were acute, told her that Alexander was telling her the truth.

"You see, Madam," he said, his tone more urgent. "I must see her again. There is no telling what lies she was told about me to get her to agree to marry Norton."

"Alexander," she said, "do you know that Mary Seton has taken religious vows?"

"Yes, Madam, I know. It was her only way to prevent a marriage she didn't want."

"I see," she said. Then: "You may accept the position."

The sun was rising over the sleeping palace as Elizabeth waited in her study for her financial ministers. When a knock came at the door, she glanced up, expecting her accountants. To her surprise, it was Dudley who entered the room and asked if he could speak to her. Her marriage negotiations with Anjou had created tension between them, but seeing him now, she marveled that the sight of him could cause her heartbeat to quicken. Surely there wasn't a handsomer man in all of Europe.

He crossed the room and knelt beside her chair. "I have come to beg your pardon. My behavior has been childish." He took her hand and kissed it. With her other hand, she touched his cheek and his hair. He might flirt with the younger and more beautiful ladies of the court, but he would always be hers.

"You forgive me?" he asked.

She said, "After the years we have known each other, what could come between us?" One of her strictest rules was that anyone who had shared her earlier years of adversity was forever entitled to her good favor.

"I was crazy with jealousy when you said you would marry Anjou."

"You should have known I could not marry a foreign

Catholic. But what other way did I have of distracting the French from thoughts of Mary Stuart?"

"Will you go on distracting all Mary Stuart's suitors with such methods?"

"As long as Mary Stuart keeps attracting suitors who will seek to destroy me, I will use whatever methods I must."

"Nothing will ever destroy you." He kissed her hand again.

She smiled again, knowing he was right. Nothing would ever destroy her, not even the attraction she felt for him. If she were not careful, she might be led to trust him as well as love him. But she was no fool. She was queen of England. Love, in her world, was a tool of statecraft and marriage a political weapon.

He must have sensed the trembly way she felt when he kissed the inside of her wrist, because he said, "You want me, my queen. I know that you do. One day you will break down and marry me."

"Maybe I will," she lied, knowing that she would always be able to refuse.

Each of her years had brought fresh lessons in the arts of survival. She had lasted this long. She could fight hostile kings and dukes. She could fight the entire Catholic world. She could fight rebellions and plots of treason. She could also fight her attraction to Dudley, which could destroy her and her kingdom as easily as anything else. Hadn't her cousin Mary of Scotland demonstrated the consequences of a queen following her heart and failing to tame her passions?

"I will wait forever," Dudley said.

She loved hearing him swear his love, but she was no fool. If she were robbed of her throne, driven from the realm as Mary Stuart had been, if she were imprisoned in a foreign land, Dudley would not journey to live with her in exile, as Alexander Beaton had done for Mary Seton.

When she didn't answer, Dudley said, "I will love you forever."

Her smile was tinged with sadness. "You will love me as

long as I am queen of England, and I will be queen of England until the day I die."

# PART IV

# MARY SETON'S STORY

"If Mary Fleming was the 'Flower of the Marys, I venture to
maintain that Mary Seton was the gem. If she wasn't the
queen's favorite, she most certainly ought to have been."
*G. Seton in his biography of the Seton Family, 1896.*

# CHAPTER 9

Tutbury Castle sat high on a hill overlooking Derbyshire, its back turned to a valley that opened up like a fan to a scattering of distant villages. From the high window of the upper chamber, one of the few rooms from which it was possible to see over the castle wall, the villages appeared quiet and idyllic, with dozens of gabled, half-timbered cottages clustered around a white-washed church. The slow, steady teams of oxen in the surrounding fields created an air of stillness, as if nothing in those villages ever changed.

Mary Seton sat in the upper chamber with the queen's other ladies, embroidering, not even listening to their whispered chatter. When Jane Kennedy, who was sitting nearest to her, reached over and touched her arm, she realized that she had dropped her needlework into her lap and had been staring out the window.

"Are you all right?" Jane whispered.

"Of course." She scooped up her embroidery and began working again. The others of the queen's companions were accustomed to Mary Seton's long silences, but Jane, who had recently arrived, still tried to pull Mary Seton into the others' chatter.

Eliza Curl, one of the queen's handmaids, came into the room and said, "Alexander Beaton is at the Shrewsbury's residence of Sheffield. He will be here before supper."

Anyone watching the group of ladies just then would have concluded that Mary Seton showed the least response. Only someone who knew her well would have noticed that she drew in her breath and seemed to sit up even straighter, working her needle with renewed energy. The others around her began talking at once, speculating on what news Alexander would bring. He had been planning to join their household earlier that month, but because of the fresh troubles in Scotland, the queen of Scots gave Alexander his first assignment: he was to return to Scotland and learn exactly what was happening there so he could tell her the news. It had been Lord Shrewsbury himself who had told the queen that her half-brother James Stuart, the Earl of Murray, had been shot by an assassin and the other lords were fighting over the regency. She thirsted for the details.

Mary Seton had long since given up on Alexander as an impossible dream. She had learned to live with the knowledge that she would never marry, and she'd grown comfortable with her quiet life in England. Gone were the days of court balls and dreams of falling in love, but gone too was the daily nightmare of Scottish rebellions and plots of treason.

With each betrayal that the queen had suffered, some flicker of hope in Mary Seton had died as well. She had watched in stunned horror as her queen fell victim to the plots of her bitterest enemies. The worst came when they suspected that Mary Fleming had helped produce the incriminating letters used against the queen. The queen, of course, protested against the accusations leveled against her cousin. "All we know is that Maitland had the letters and Mary Fleming may have seen them. All we can hold her responsible for is not denouncing them as forgeries." But they had all learned handwriting from the same French masters. How many people were there in Scotland capable of writing French and forging the queen's writing?

Mary Seton had learned to ease the pain by retreating into herself. She liked remembering the river that ran behind the stone convent walls of the Convent of St. Pierre, and the fragrant beauty of the gardens in bloom. She remembered the bluffs, overgrown with vegetation that hung over the river and the delicate blue speckled eggs tucked in a nest in the crevice of the heavy bark. She could almost breathe the sweet delicious small of the wet earth. She had already made arrangements to enter the convent when the queen no longer needed her. The convent meant freedom now, as it had once meant escape from the confines of the French court.

She had known all along that her place was far away from a world where the lust for power made possible such lies as she had seen. She liked knowing that somewhere, far away, the gates of the convent gardens enclosed a beautiful world remote from Scottish rebellions and English intrigues. She drew comfort from the knowledge that the convent gardens were always there, waiting for her.

The others were talking about what news Alexander Beaton would bring. Perhaps he had learned who would be the next regent. Perhaps he had even learned who had assassinated James Stuart. The queen of Scots planned to reward whoever had done the deed.

Mary Seton set aside her embroidery, and very quietly said, "Please excuse me. I must rest for awhile."

This was so typical of her that the others didn't give her more than a passing glance. She walked down the curved staircase which led from the upper rooms and then went into the bedroom she shared with two of the queen's other attendants. The hazy sunshine slanting in through the high windows lit the gray walls so they glowed like silver. From the wardrobe she removed a heavy pewter casket containing her personal treasures and she reread the letters Alexander had written her.

His letters were full of apologies for having let her down. He wrote of her brother's promise to have him killed if he interfered with the family's marriage negotiations. "Your brother is a real terror," he wrote. "If the Setons had been guarding the queen instead of the Douglas family, she would still be locked up on that island." In another letter he wrote: "The trick, I suppose, is to do just what you have done: Pretend to go along with their plans but find ways to get what you want."

But she understood now how wrong her approach had been. Looking back, she understood her strategy had been about avoiding trouble, avoiding confrontation, and waiting for her chance to escape. At the time it seemed like a good idea to pretend she would indeed marry Norton while doing all she could to postpone the wedding.

The problem with the approach was it was dishonest. While pretending and avoiding, she had sacrificed something of herself. There could never be any joy in that kind of victory. The only way to win the game was to refuse to play at all.

She had been able to smuggle only one letter out to him. She told him that he had nothing to apologize for. She also told him that she was happy with her decision to take religions vows.

She laid down on her bed, closing the curtains to block out the foul smell which, when the wind shifted south, came up from the marshlands to the rear of the castle. She must have drifted into a light sleep because when she heard heavy footsteps walking along the corridor leading to the upper rooms, she knew that Alexander had arrived.

She stood up and went to the bronze mirror mounted over the cupboard on the far side of the room. After tucking stray stands of hair into her cap, she splashed water from the basin onto her face, the cold water turning her cheeks a lively pink. In a moment of rare vanity, she removed her plain gray cap and replaced it with a black velvet heart-shaped cap embroidered with silver, and drew a finely woven black shawl over her shoulders.

The queen and her ladies had moved into the room which served as her reception chamber. The queen sat, facing Alexander, who stood with the handful of riders who had accompanied him. Melville, the queen's secretary and ambassador to the English court, stood near the window. Alexander's back was to her, but she recognized him from the thickness of his curls and the familiar square of his back.

In that moment, Mary Seton shared the queen's feeling of indignity at the conditions of her prison. Here were no glittering gold mirrors or finely polished paneling of the French court or even the tapestries and polished wooden furnishing of Holyrood. This room contained only the queen's high-backed chair, upholstered with purple velvet, over which was mounted her gold cloth of state embossed with the royal arms of Scotland. The queen's few touches of luxury served only to emphasize the chilly emptiness of the room.

The queen was saying, "I'm always happy to welcome any kin of my faithful ambassador the archbishop. Now tell me what is happening in my realm."

Mary Seton crossed the room to stand beside the queen, knowing Alexander was watching her. She was glad that when she took her place beside the queen, he merely nodded at her and said, "Greetings, Lady Mary." She was grateful to him for his formality. Their first meeting after all these years was too special to her to want to show the others anything except strict formality. Later, in private, away from the curiosity of the others, they could talk.

To the queen, he said, "Before your brother was murdered, he tried to prove that his mother had been legally married to your father the king and that the crown was therefore his. He and Maitland quarreled over this. So many people were furious at him for trying to take the crown that he could have been assassinated by any number of people, but most people believe it was a Hamilton."

"What is Seton doing?" the queen asked. "And Huntly?"

"Maitland and Huntly are holding the Castle of Edinburgh in your name. Seton is in France, gathering Catholic support for your cause."

"There will be war again," she said. "They will fight over the regency."

"Maybe not," said Alexander. "The English are planning to intervene to prevent civil war in Scotland. They're afraid civil war will bring in the French or Spanish."

To Melville, she said, "We must write to Elizabeth right away." She turned to Willie Douglas, who served as her page. "Please show Alexander to his room and help him get settled. He must be exhausted from the journey."

With just a quick look at Mary Seton, Alexander followed Willie from the room.

Instead of returning to the upper chamber to spend the remainder of the afternoon with the others, Mary Seton again excused herself and went to the castle's inner courtyard. The enclosed courtyard was no more than twenty paces across, shaded by six fully grown apple trees. At times direct sunlight filtered through the branches casting dappled shadows across the stone walkway, but now the skies were overcast. She sat on the courtyard's only bench, knowing that Alexander would soon find her here. He would ask Willie where she had gone, and Willie would tell him that this was where she always came for fresh air.

During the three quarters of an hour that she waited for him, she felt remarkably calm. So many times during the years since she had seen him, she had imagined what they would say to each other should they ever again meet, but now her mind was strangely blank. How long ago it seemed, when she snuck from Holyrood to spend days with him. As full of romantic dreams as she had been then, she never could have predicted that he would journey so far and work so diligently just to be able to see her again. Never could she have predicted that he would prove so constant. She didn't like thinking that now she might have to disappoint him.

When she heard the door rattle and open, she wanted to jump to her feet. Instead she sat still, watching Alexander as he walked toward her, marveling at the familiarity of his face, a perfect oval except for the square of his jaw. How odd that she should feel she had just seen him yesterday, as if no time had passed since the day he had bid her farewell at the gates of Holyrood. She felt as if she could have drawn every line of his face and crinkle around his eyes from memory.

He smiled. "Hello."

"Hello," she said, smiling back. Could it be as simple as that?

He sat beside her. As he searched her face, an odd shyness came over her and she found it difficult to look at him.

He touched the locket at her waist. "You still wear her picture?"

She opened the locket to show him the portrait of the queen which had been painted just before her wedding to the dauphin. "She doesn't smile like that anymore," she said.

"She has changed," Alexander said. "For a moment I couldn't believe it was her. She seems different, so serious, even somber. I always remember her high-spirits and laughter. You have changed, too. You used to try to hide your thoughts. Now you do. Your face is completely unreadable."

"I feel like a different person."

"You remind me of one of those Italian paintings of the smiling angels so far removed from earthly concerns."

She was surprised by how accurate his guess was. There was so much she had to explain to him. "I always expected to see you again," she said. "Especially when we were still in Scotland. Whenever there were crowds, I looked for you. I even looked for you that day in Edinburgh when she signed her abdication. But I never expected you to come back like this."

"I knew I'd come back. Through every change in the queen's fortunes, I asked about you and the answer was always the same: Mary of the proud Setons is still by the queen's side. I knew you were behind her when she was dragged through the streets of Edinburgh and I knew you were in the fishing boat when she escaped Scotland."

Mary Seton was fully aware of what people said about her: they said she was the most devout and loyal of the queen's ladies, the only one who had remained with the queen constantly, through the years of pain as well as the years of joy. She felt she didn't deserve such high praise. Her life had never offered her any real choices.

"I remember why I first loved you," he said. "You seemed so unattainable, so untouchable, so highly placed at the French court, but I felt that I alone understood you. I wanted to rescue you from the life you hated. I had the romantic idea that rescuing you would make me worthy of your love."

She smiled. "I first loved you at the queen's wedding when you mocked everything about the court. I never dared do that."

"But I let you down."

"You couldn't have helped any of it. I know that." But she could see from his frown that he didn't accept all that had happened as inevitable, as she did.

"There's something I don't understand," he said. "If she can smuggle letters in and out, why doesn't she try to escape?"

"She has no wish to wander around the English countryside without a major power to back her. This isn't Lochleven with my brother's army waiting for on the other side of the lake. She'll have to wait for help from the Spanish or the French."

"It's a dangerous game," Alexander said.

"Too many times since we've come to England, I've seen her hopes raised and crushed. I hate watching each disappointment hurt her as if it's the first. Elizabeth Tudor has done some astonishing things. I believe her capable of anything."

Alexander looked away and said, "That wasn't the

impression I had of her. She seemed sad, full of nervous energy like a hummingbird, and afraid."

"I trust you'll forgive me if I don't pity the queen of England." She kicked at a clump of dried leaves near her feet, and then said, "Did you know that Christopher Norton was executed after the Northern Rebellion?"

"Yes, and I knew your family was arranging another marriage for you."

"They wanted me to marry his younger brother, Robert. Do you know that I have taken religious vows?"

"It is possible to release you from those. I spent enough time in the church to know that."

She shook her head and turned away, wondering if she could explain what the vows meant to her and why she could not renounce them.

"Mary? Tell me."

"Everything changed after I took the vows," she said.

"Of course everything changed. Nobody could force you to marry."

"It was more than that." Never before had she tried to describe the emotions she had felt when she had finally decided to take religious vows. "I used to feel bitter and angry, but after taking the vows, I no longer felt that I lived in a prison. In my heart, I already lived in the sunny convent."

"There are other alternatives," he insisted, "to prison or the convent."

She smiled, but her smile was sad because she knew that he still didn't understand. "I went to a lot of trouble to convince everyone that all along my secret had been my devout Catholicism. At first my family didn't believe me. They had found your letters to me, after all. But I convinced them that you had written such things to me, but I had never wanted anything other than a religious life." She touched his hand, letting her hand rest on his. "I took the coward's way by telling a lie. I don't expect you to forgive me for that."

"Of course I forgive you. You were trapped and had to

lie."

"The lie bought my freedom. It assures me, at any time, of a means of escape. If I renounce my vows, I lose that protection. If I renounce my vows and something happens to you, I am again at the mercy of the changing winds of politics and fortune The only thing that guarantees my freedom for the rest of my life is to hold onto my vows."

"If you marry me, you will be free from the changing winds of politics and fortune."

She didn't answer, but she saw his face grow troubled, his frown deepen, and she knew that now he understood. As much as the queen of England insisted that they lived in honorable guardianship the fact was that this was a prison and the queen of Scots and her entire household was entirely powerless.

"You're afraid," he said quietly. "I understand that. You are afraid to tie your fortunes with mine. But I'll find a way to offer you protection for as long as you live."

She smiled, moved and surprised by the bravado in his voice. She felt much older than him, as if the hellish years she had lived through in Scotland had aged her, making her cynical and wary. Soon, though, he would understand the futility of his hopes. If she renounced her vows without a proper dispensation, there would be scandal, and no Catholic country would recognize their marriage. Even if she could obtain a dispensation from her vows, they had no livelihood. The queen was no longer able to bestow manors on her favorites, as she had done for Mary Livingston.

"We just need time," he said, lifting her hand and kissing her palm.

She made an effort to smile when she said, "Here, at least, we have plenty of time."

# CHAPTER 10

Mary Seton stood at a window on the landing of the staircase, looking into the stormy, overcast sky, so gray and dark against the bright, dying leaves of autumn. Startled by the feel of a hand on her shoulder, she turned around.

The queen said, "Is Alexander Beaton the man you had me write a letter for a long time ago?"

"Yes. You remember."

"I am guilty of taking your friendship for granted, of being so consumed by my own troubles that I neglect my closest friends, but of course I remember. I also notice that you have often smiled since Alexander Beaton has arrived. I've known you to smile so rarely."

Mary Seton felt such love for the queen at that moment, a love mixed with her returning affections for Alexander, that she wanted to throw her arms around the queen and kiss her. But years of stifling her emotions made her uncomfortable with such spontaneity.

"Alexander has spoken to me," the queen said, "and I have promised to help him. If you refuse to look out for your own happiness, than I will have to do it for you. Shall I go through all my years so preoccupied with my own misery that I pay no attention to the misery of my most devoted friends?"

"I am not miserable."

"When have you ever known any real joy, as I have? When I married the dauphin and became queen of France, I may have been so happy that I used up my lifetime allotment of happiness. But as far as I can see, you have never had any joy in your life."

The truth of the queen's words came as a fresh surprise. "Nothing turned out quite as we planned, did it?"

"I believe you should marry Alexander Beaton."

"But my vows!"

"Those are a problem, of course. Even if we find a way to absolve you of your vows, your family will still be a problem. The Setons are proud. Your grandmother's fondest wish was that you would marry as well as your brothers. And your brother has been so loyal to me, it will be difficult to go against his wishes, but you have been just as loyal, and your happiness is dearer to me than my own."

"There is simply nothing we can do now," said Mary Seton.

"But there is." The queen took her hands. "I will write to my cousin the cardinal for advice about your vows, and I will think more about the problem. Even if we get your vows annulled, you still can't marry Alexander because of his low rank. Therefore I have decided to raise his rank. His family has earned the honor many times over, and a noble rank would make him a suitable bridegroom for a daughter of Lord Seton."

Mary Seton knew her astonishment showed in her face because the queen, seeing her expression, smiled happily. "What excuse do you have now for refusing your noble suitor?"

"Did Alexander accept the promotion?" She rather enjoyed the idea of Alexander, who had once mocked everything about court life, given a title.

"He was willing to accept the title if it would help you and your family accept him as your husband. Surely even your proud family will accept a noble son of the Beatons."

Would they? Mary Seton smiled, remembering that George had once threatened to murder Alexander if he interfered in their plans for her. For a moment she let herself imagine what George would say if, after all that had happened, she married Alexander Beaton. She had forgotten how wonderfully defiant she had felt in Edinburgh when she had escaped to spend afternoons with Alexander. Some of the hopelessness that had built up over the years fell away as she imagined her brother's face when he heard the news.

Mary Seton kissed the queen's hand. "The world has never seen a more generous queen or a truer friend."

That evening, she and Alexander sat together on the bench in the inner courtyard. Quietly she said, "Has anyone thought about the meaningless of the queen's offer? The government in Scotland is founded on the claim that her abdication is binding. You will be a nobleman without lands, your estate bestowed by a queen without a country."

Alexander smiled as if amused by the whole idea. "But the Setons will recognize my rank. As good Catholics, they not only consider her queen of Scotland, but rightful queen of England as well."

"I received a letter from Mary Livingston today. Rumor does travel fast."

"What does she say?"

"She says I should forsake my vows, even if I must become a Protestant to do it. She also told me not to worry about what other people will say. She never did."

"Mary Livingston's advice sounds wise to me."

"Mary Livingston was never trapped by her family. She doesn't know how it feels to hold on to her one avenue to freedom."

As if to prove himself worthy of his new rank, Alexander began taking risks to smuggle the queen's messages from the castle. As the turmoil in Scotland moved toward another civil war, the queen's household centered around the receiving and sending of letters. It was becoming more and more difficult to exchange letters with the people on the continent. The pirates swarming the English Channel made travel nearly impossible.

"They say queen Elizabeth encourages the pirates," said one of the queen's ladies.

"Of course she does," said Alexander. "Everyone knows that. She can't afford a full scale navy, and the pirates protect her shores. Whenever a Spanish ship gets too close, the pirates attack. Philip of Spain demands the English queen to punish the outlaws, but I think she secretly rewards them. The pirates are certainly growing rich from Spanish plunder. And no English flagship has ever been attacked by pirates."

"What kind of queen would encourage pirates as a means of statecraft?" said the Scottish queen.

"A cunning woman who will stoop to any means to achieve her goals," said Alexander. "We have a formidable enemy."

The queen's smuggled letters went out with the wash and tucked into the binding of books. The queen devised excuses to send her servants to the neighboring towns. Throughout the winter months, Alexander and Gilbert Curl, her steward, traveled throughout Derbyshire and Staffordshire.

Watching Alexander smuggling letters made Mary Seton uneasy. "Do you remember what happened to those who were arrested after the Norfolk marriage talks?"

"They were caught," he said. "I won't be." Seeing that Mary Seton was truly anxious, he said, "Helping her escape from this unjust prison is the right thing to do, you know that."

"The English tortured Herries' men for information before Norfolk was executed," Mary Seton said. "Queen Elizabeth shows no mercy to those who work on behalf of our queen.

So many have died already."

"I can't pretend I don't have a selfish motive as well. If she's returned to her throne, there would be nothing to stop us from marrying."

This, she knew, was true enough even though she didn't believe the queen would either escape or be restored to her throne.

The next time Alexander returned from Staffordshire, he returned with a letter from Mary Fleming. Mary Seton was sitting beside the queen in the sunny upper chamber when Alexander brought the letter in. The queen gestured for Mary Seton to take it.

Mary Seton broke the seal and read: "My dearest and most beloved queen and cousin: I beg you with all my heart to forgive my husband his past follies. I suffer, knowing you can never forgive me. God punishes me daily with pain and grief and shame for having doubted that in time you would triumph over your enemies. Soon there will be war again. Maitland is holding the Castle of Edinburgh in your name. He will fight to the death for you, to avenge all past wrongs."

Mary Seton knew that Mary Fleming had been crying as she wrote. It was hard to imagine the vibrant Mary Fleming crying, just as it was hard to imagine her humbled and sorry.

"Write back to her for me," said the queen. "Tell her I forgive her completely. It hardly matters any more, and she has a heavy enough weight to carry. Will you write the letter for me?"

"I will." Mary Seton wrote the letter that afternoon.

How scattered the four Marys were now: Mary Beaton was living on her husband's French estates, Mary Fleming was in war-torn Edinburgh as Maitland prepared to defend the queen, and Mary Livingston, who journeyed regularly to England to visit them, was living a quiet life in the west of Scotland with her children.

An official envoy arrived from London to inform the

queen of Scots that the fighting in Scotland had ended. Maitland, Huntly, and Hamilton had been defeated, Lennox had been assassinated, and the Earl of Mar now controlled the regency. When the queen heard the news, she fell into a fit of melancholia and weeping, which reminded Mary Seton of her state of mind after Darnley's murder. For days she remained in bed, hot with fever, complaining of a pain in her side. Only Mary Seton appreciated the full force of this news: The Earl of Mar, who was now in control of Scotland, had been one of the lords who planned Riccio's murder.

This was bad enough, but Alexander smuggled in letters from Scotland informing them that Mar had won the battle with the help of English aid offered by Queen Elizabeth's government. Nobody dared tell the queen this while she was feverish and ill, but when she recovered a bit, she began asking for news, demanding that nothing be kept from her. The others decided that Mary Seton should tell her. "You were with her through all the trouble that Mar caused," Jane Kennedy said. "She should hear it from you."

Mary Seton entered the queen's private room and sat on a low wooden stool beside the bed. The queen's eyes were closed, her skin pasty-white. She breathed so faintly that for a frightening moment, Mary Seton thought she was dying. When the queen opened her eyes and tried to speak, no words came. Mary Seton handed her a water goblet from the nearby table and helped her drink.

When she could speak, she said, "You have some news. There is something you know."

Mary Seton said, "The fighting has ended completely in Scotland. Mar is regent."

"Did Elizabeth support him?"

Mary Seton returned the goblet to the table. "I don't know why she wanted him to be the next regent," she said, "but she did."

"She favored him because he has been in her pay all these years. So now, with Queen Elizabeth's help, the Earl of Mar has my crown."

"There is nothing more you can expect from Elizabeth Tudor. They say that she insists on constant pomp and ceremony, that she shuns any familiarity between herself and her attendants, that she never shows anyone her real face. It's impossible to make peace with someone who puts so many barriers between herself and the rest of the world."

"Why can't she see that since childhood our families and advisors have been trying to poison us against each other? Why can't she rise above that?"

"Because she is cruel and unfeeling, interested only in power and personal victory whatever the cost."

For a long time the queen was quiet, breathing heavily. Mary thought she was asleep. Then she said, "She may keep me locked in this castle, she may even take my life, but she can never rob me of the truth I carry in my heart. She incited the Reformation in Scotland and since then she has constantly aided my rebels against me. She lured me into England on false promises of help and has imprisoned me ever since. Surely she realizes that history will judge her harshly."

"She pretends that she acts at the demand of her people and ministers," said Mary Seton. "She thinks everyone believes her theatrics."

"They may believe her now, but later we will have the same judge, and how will she defend herself? Now, I want to talk of something other than the queen of England. Have we received a response yet from the cardinal?"

"Not yet.

"Alexander Beaton would make a fine husband. He's principled, and brave, and honest. I cannot find fault with him at all. I understand why you love him. I always intended to give you whatever you wanted, to make you happy. Now I can see that because of me you've given up so much."

"That isn't true."

"But I will make it up to you now, I promise."

Three days later, a letter arrived from the cardinal saying that Mary Seton's vows could be annulled, but obtaining the dispensation would require a trip to Rome. Because the trip was so dangerous, Mary Seton assumed that this would put an end to talk of annulling her vows.

At the same time a smuggled letter written in cipher came from Rome detailing another plot on the continent. King Philip of Spain's half-brother, Don John of Austria, wanted to try to rescue the Scottish queen, and the Pope endorsed his plan. Don John, who had recently won the battle of Lepanto against the infidels who were spreading into Europe from the Mediterranean, was the darling of the Catholic world. The only thing Don John lacked now was a crown, and the way he saw of obtaining one was to rescue and marry the queen of Scotland. Such plotting was dangerous, but Mary Seton had learned a long time ago not to try to keep the queen of Scots from corresponding with those who wished to rescue her. The only thing that made the queen's time in prison bearable was the hope that one day she would be rescued and her dignity in the eyes of the world would be restored.

When Alexander gallantly offered to journey to Rome to obtain Mary Seton's dispensation himself, and at the same time meet with Don John on behalf of the queen of Scots, Mary Seton turned cold with fear.

She sensed that all protestations would be in vain, but she had to try. When they were alone together, she said, "The entire plan is foolish. If you dodge the pirates, the English will catch you and torture you. Why must I always be forced to watch the people I love rush headlong into danger?"

"Remember that I faced Queen Elizabeth. After that, I can have no fear of pirates."

"You're joking and this is serious. I can keep you from going. I'll refuse to marry you, even if you get the dispensation."

"I'll go anyway. I can see right now that if I don't, I'll sit in this castle waiting forever. Maybe you've gotten used to a life without hope, but I haven't."

"I'd rather have you here, and alive."

"It's time for me to be heroic. I wasn't very heroic when I was helpless against your brother, but now there's something I can do to make up for the lost years."

"I remember the last time you left for Rome. You said you'd be back by winter. You never came back."

"This time you know I will."

In early spring, as soon as the weather permitted travel, Alexander prepared for his journey to the Continent. The English, who were predictably suspicious of his journey, refused to guarantee his safety.

Mary Seton stood alone in the upper chamber, watching as he and his small troop of horsemen galloped away, disappearing into the distant hills. For the first time in years, Mary Seton felt the intensity of longing for something. She wished she could write to him, but all she could do was wait for his return. She had never had the courage to tell her family the truth, but when he came back, she would redeem her integrity and for the first time tell her family the truth that was in her heart.

The first afternoon he was gone, Bess Shrewsbury, their jailer's wife, joined them with gossip interesting enough to get Mary Seton's mind off Alexander and his journey. Bess often amused the Scottish queen by imitating the way Queen Elizabeth strutted around like a man, shouting at her advisors, hitting them with her fan when they angered her.

"The news which has the English court in an uproar is about Robert Dudley," said Bess, "the queen's favorite. Everyone says he's been her lover for years," Bess paused dramatically, enjoying the rapt attention of her audience. "Yesterday he got married. He married Lettice Knollys, Francis Knollys' youngest daughter, only nineteen and easily the most beautiful girl at the English court."

"The English queen must have been furious," said the

queen of Scots.

Bess laughed. "She threw a fit like the court has never seen. She was ready to clap both Dudley and Lettice into the Tower, but Cecil can somehow calm her temper. He convinced her that she had no grounds to imprison them. She forbid Lettice to ever come into her presence and she has sent Dudley away from the court."

The queen said, "She has no shame, throwing such a jealous fit in front of the entire court."

"She may love him," Jane Kennedy said, "but she'll never love anyone enough to want to share her crown."

Mary Seton wondered if Queen Elizabeth really and truly loved Robert Dudley. Everyone said that she did, that she actually blushed like a young girl whenever he was around, but Mary Seton found it difficult to reconcile the image of the blushing and love-struck English queen with the calculating and ruthless ruler she had proven herself to be. She found it similarly difficult to reconcile the image in her portraits, frail, thin, and timid, with the stories about how she bullied her advisors and ministers. Even Alexander's assessment of her seemed full of contradictions. Could it be that Elizabeth Tudor, who had her way absolutely, who played a game of cat-and-mouse with the trusting and naive queen of Scots, was unhappy and frustrated in love?

Two weeks passed before a letter from Alexander was smuggled into the Scottish queen's household. His letter was written in cipher, as were all the letters which the queen wrote and received. He wrote that on his way to Rome, he had stopped for a visit with Don John and had distressing news to report: Don John was forced to temporarily abandon his plans to rescue the queen of Scots. He had been taken by surprise by a Protestant rebellion in his province of Flanders, and putting down the rebellion was consuming all his energy. He suspected, but could not prove, that Queen Elizabeth's government had funded the rebels.

"For once Elizabeth is becoming predictable," the queen said. "Since she knows Don John will never consider marrying her, she enacts her second-choice plan of stirring up rebellion among his subjects!"

The next letter from Alexander arrived the following week. "I have obtained the dispensation," he wrote to Mary Seton, "and I am understandably eager to return to England. I have also been to the Convent of St. Pierre. I see why you love it, Mary. I walked through the gardens and by the river you spoke of. It's perfectly lovely."

She received letters from her family as well. They had heard the rumors about a romance, and they begged her to announce that the stories were false. She didn't answer their letters. A new feeling of lightness came over her and she was ashamed of her former bitterness and anger.

One afternoon she looked from the window of the upper chamber and saw a small troop of horsemen approaching the castle. She knew it couldn't be Alexander yet. Had he arrived in England, she would have heard from him. Sometime later she looked up to see Jane Kennedy standing in the doorway. "Who were the horsemen?" she asked.

"They spoke to the queen," Jane said. "Go into her room. She will tell you."

The queen was ill again. For days she had been in bed, feverish. Mary Seton entered her room, pushed the bed curtains open a crack, and knelt beside the bed. The queen reached for her hand. "My dear Mary Seton."

The windows were sealed shut against the stench fumes from the marshlands, so the air inside was close and warm.

"You are so hot," Mary Seton said.

"I feel better." In this dim light, her eyes were the exact color her hair used to be, before losing its youthful glossiness, a warm, glowing brown tinged with golden amber.

"Jane didn't tell you?"

"Tell me what?" asked Mary Seton.

The queen whispered, "My dear Mary, Alexander's ship

was attacked by English pirates. He was buried at sea."

Mary Seton didn't now how she came to be alone again, how she excused herself from the queen and came to be in her own room.

Needing absolute privacy, she drew her bed curtains closed, shutting out even the dim light that came from the cracks in the window shutters. She cursed the queen of England's deplorable, cowardly policy of encouraging the pirates. What kind of ridiculous, ruthless idea was it to encourage piracy as a means of national defense? It had been Elizabeth, as surely as it had been the pirates, who had murdered Alexander. And it was just like the queen of England that the deed was done so that she appeared blameless. Had Alexander been caught, had he been brought to the Tower and tortured for information about the Don John plot, had he been executed for treason against the English crown, everyone would see the blood on Elizabeth Tudor's hands.

In her anger and grief, Mary Seton didn't doubt that Queen Elizabeth Tudor, who probably knew that Alexander had been returning from a meeting with Don John, had been happy about his death. Alexander had insisted that he had found the queen of England sympathetic and easily moved, but Mary Seton concluded that Alexander, being full of goodness himself, saw only goodness in others. If Elizabeth Tudor was a living example of what it was to constantly fight against the world, Mary Seton wanted no part of it.

During the hours and days that followed, Mary Seton's only visitors were Jane Kennedy, who brought her food on a tray, and the queen herself, who frequently came to sit with her and hold her hands. As Mary Seton mourned Alexander, she mourned the dreams of her childhood which would never come true, and she grieved for all that had been impossible for her. But at least she knew now that Alexander's kind of love was possible. Had their lives not been completely entwined in politics, had her destiny, like her queen's, not been linked with the losing cause of Catholicism, she and Alexander may have found happiness.

She considered leaving Tutbury and retiring to the convent early, but she knew that she couldn't yet leave her queen, who for so many years had been the central focus of her life. In the dark days immediately following Alexander's death, she did as her family wished and assured them that she had never intended to marry Alexander Beaton. What did it matter? She had always lied to them anyway, and this last brought them comfort. She had nothing to fear from them anymore. She had never renounced her vows, so she was protected. She didn't belong to their world. They could no longer use her as a pawn in their struggle for power.

Several weeks later, when she emerged from her strict mourning, ready to take her place again in the sunny upper chamber embroidering with the others, everyone noticed a change in her, a new peacefulness about her. She was, as Alexander had said, like an angel in an Italian painting smiling serenely upon earthly concerns which could no longer hurt her.

# CHAPTER 11

The days and weeks passed quickly for Mary Seton now,
for there was nothing to set one day apart from the next. The
only change from day to day was the queen's fluctuating
health. Mary Seton's family sent regular reports of her many
nieces and nephews, many of whom were now approaching
adulthood. When George fell ill with pox and was not
expected to live much longer, Mary Seton dutifully wrote,
expressing her grief. When she received word of his death, she
went through the proper mourning rituals. She had resented
him for standing in the way of all that she wanted, but in her
newly found peace, she wondered what kind of brother he
might have been, had they lived in another era, out from
under the shadow of family ambition and politics. As she
knelt with the queen's secret priest and said the necessary
prayers for his soul, she felt pity that he had failed in his life's
ambition to better the position of the Seton family. Indeed,
during his lifetime, the Setons, allied as they were to the
blighted queen of Scots, had fallen considerably in wealth and

power.

One of Mary's nephews was the same age as Prince James, Mary Stuart's son. George's oldest son, now the Premier Baron of Scotland, was trying to have him included among the prince's companions. She remembered her own grandmother using every influence she had to get Mary Seton included among the young Scottish queen's companions, when Mary was five years old. Mary Seton sighed, thinking that the cycle would begin again, but now she was far away from it all.

Some years were filled with hope: Perhaps it was a plan on the continent to rescue the queen of Scots, or perhaps Queen Elizabeth reopened negotiations for restoring the queen of Scots to her throne, but nothing came of any of the plans.

With each disappointment, the queen of Scots seemed to age a bit more. The worst disappointment came when she found out what kind of man her son was growing into. She knew, of course, that he had been raised by her enemies and taught to regard her as the murderer of his father, but she always expected the natural love of a son for his mother to overcome all else. But his only concern was to please the queen of England so she would recognize him as her heir. He never made more than a half-hearted attempt to restore his mother to her former glory.

The Scottish queen's hair became thinner and whitened. Her waist thickened. Her legs were often swollen with her illness and her skin was yellowish. When her health was good enough, she was allowed to go out riding, surrounded by what Shrewsbury called an honorable escort, but was in truth a small army. Sometimes Mary Seton opened her locket, where she kept Alexander's picture beside the queen's, and she hurt for the once-beautiful queen who had thought she could rule Scotland with nothing but charm and personal grace.

Mary Seton knew that she, also, was changing, her posture becoming more rigid, her voice chillier. She'd always been slender, but now her bones were fragile, her long fingers no longer nimble. Years of living in close confinement made the queen and Mary Seton more alike: The queen not only seemed comfortable with Mary Seton's silences, but occasionally, when she wanted to sit quietly with one who understood her completely, loved her absolutely, and felt no need for a constant stream of conversation, she even preferred Mary Seton's somber company to the lively gossip of the others.

Eighteen years after they had come to England, it appeared that the long-awaited rescue of the Scottish queen would come at last. Philip of Spain was building the Armada, consisting of one hundred twenty five ships, one thousand long-range guns, and twenty eight thousand soldiers. Spain had long been the mightiest world power and now the king of Spain was building the Armada with one chief aim: To defeat queen Elizabeth of England and restore Catholic power in Europe. England, a small insignificant country in comparison, couldn't hope to withstand the Armada. The Scottish queen's young cousin, the new Duke of Guise, grown now to manhood, offered a reward of two thousand pounds – an enormous sum of money – to any assassin who could "rid the world of that heretic Elizabeth."

The end was drawing near, and Mary Seton knew it. Philip of Spain and Elizabeth of England were moving toward war, and the fate of Mary Queen of Scots hung in the balance. The queen of Scots understood that everything she said in front of witnesses, even if just Bess Shrewsbury or one of the guards, was talked about, even published abroad. She was therefore careful with everything she said, and sometimes at night, wrote out what she would say the next day, particularly if there were messengers from the English court.

She told Bess Shrewsbury, "I've given up all dreams but one. I want only the chance to speak for myself in public. I once dreamed of reigning over three nations, marrying the heir to Spain as I had married the heir of France. Now all I want is to regain my dignity and tell the world how I have suffered for Catholicism."

These were her public words, but Mary Seton knew that should Philip of Spain triumph over the English, Elizabeth Tudor would be imprisoned as a Protestant usurper of the English throne. After years of resentment against Queen Elizabeth's double-crossing politics, the queen of Scots would rejoice to see the tables turned, their places reversed.

One morning just before the Scottish queen's household held their secret Mass, the castle entrance clanged open. One of the queen's handmaids rushed in to say that a troop of riders had arrived from the royal court. There was a rush of activity as Jane Kennedy locked the queen's cupboards, Eliza Curl hid the chest containing the queen's jewels in her wardrobe, and the queen herself threw the codes for her cipher into the softly crackling fire.

The door was flung open and several Englishmen stood on the threshold. "How dare you storm my private rooms?" the queen demanded.

A tall gangly man with a long pointed black beard who was evidently the leader stepped forward and said, "My name is Francis Walsingham. I am here by order of Queen Elizabeth." He extended a piece of parchment from which dangled the gold wax of the royal seal. "We have been given orders to search your rooms. If you refuse to unlock these cupboards, we will have to break them open."

The queen drew herself up to full height and said, "Jane, open the cupboards for these gentlemen."

Walsingham pulled out a bundle of smuggled letters and shuffled through them. He then unfolded the list of English families who had pledged their support to Mary Stuart should something happen to Elizabeth Tudor.

The queen stepped forward and said quietly, "Leave that list here. The families on the list are innocent. The guilt is mine."

"I have no doubt about that," said Walsingham. "But the list must be shown to the queen of England so she can see how many of her subjects you have seduced from their loyalty."

When Walsingham and his men left, the queen's household was in gloom, but the queen herself was cheerful, even buoyant. "They must be worried about Philip and the Armada," she said, "or they should not be going to such lengths now. Rescue must be close."

Mary Seton marveled at her energy, her unfailingly high hopes, her optimism.

A few days after Walsingham left, Queen Elizabeth announced that something had to be done about the Scottish queen's lax guardianship. Nobody ever mentioned prisons or jailers, as if calling Shrewsbury a guardian fooled the world. When the English council announced that the Scottish queen's next guardian would be sir Amyas Paulet, Mary Seton felt the queen was doomed. Paulet, a staunch Puritan who was fiercely devoted to Queen Elizabeth, had been one of the Scottish queen's most outspoken enemies for years.

His first day as her guardian, Paulet strode into the queen's antechamber and, without even waiting for her to speak first, as etiquette demanded, he said, "You must remove that cloth of state."

"I must?" asked the queen calmly. "And who are you to say *must* to a sovereign?"

"I shall speak any way I wish to a Catholic adulteress and murderess. Official permission has never been given for you to set up a farcical symbol of authority. The cloth of state must come down."

Because none of the queen's servants would move to take down the cloth, Paulet had to bring in his own men to take it down. Mary Seton watched Paulet as he supervised the removal of the cloth. No more than thirty years old, Paulet had been a child when the Scottish queen first arrived in England and all he knew of her were the stories and rumors and accusations. He fully believed that the Scottish queen had murdered Darnley so she could marry her lover Bothwell.

After he left, the queen said, "If he thinks I can be wounded by such pettiness after all I have endured he is sadly mistaken. Willie, please mount my crucifix over my chair."

The next day when Paulet returned, she greeted him with a calm smile, seated beneath the crucifix. "You can rob me of my earthly sovereignty," she said, "you can force me to endure every possible humiliation. You can even take away my life. But you can never remove the truth that is in my heart."

After that it became a battle of nerves. Paulet was fond of saying, "What is a queen who has disgraced her calling? Who shall bow to a woman who has brought shame to her nation?" The queen took to writing out her statements the evening before so that she could recite them exactly for Paulet.

Paulet tightened the castle security. Every book, every basket of laundry, and the sole of every shoe that passed through the gates was searched. The endless stream of messages that had kept the queen's hopes alive dried up.

Mary Seton, thoroughly disgusted by Paulet, had at first spurned the friendship of his daughter, Clare. The queen herself, who loved the company of children, was now far too preoccupied with the coming of the Spanish Armada to pay attention to the young girl. But as the security around them tightened and it became more and more difficult to communicate with the outside world, Mary Seton came to depend on Clare to keep them informed of what was happening.

She found Clare's eagerness for stories delightful rather than annoying and tiresome. Clare begged to hear about the queen's exciting life – all events which had happened before she was born. Oddly enough, Mary Seton enjoyed recounting the stories, telling her how the queen had been plotted against, how she had outsmarted Darnley the night of Riccio's murder, and how Willie had stolen the keys from Lord Douglas.

It was satisfying to set the record straight, even if just for one romantic, starry-eyed girl.

# Destiny

After many months of being cut off from the outside world, the queen's household was moved to Fotheringhay Castle. For so long they'd had no way to communicate with the outside world except through Paulet. Then at last, one of the queen's servants, Clifford, found a way to penetrate Paulet's strict guard: the brewer who each week brought a keg of ale hid letters in the bung-hole of the keg. Letters were exchanged weekly between the queen of Scots and Gifford, who in turn passed her letters on to the French embassy, the Guises, the Pope, and Spain. This way the queen's household learned that the Armada was building in strength. They learned that Queen Elizabeth's government, panicked, published pamphlets calling on all loyal subjects to join the royal navy. The Pope announced that the Catholic world held Mary Queen of Scots as the finest example of faith and devotion.

It was a triumph for her. The word was being spread that she was something other than an adulteress and murderess. At last the truth would be published abroad.

One day Paulet entered the queen's apartments and told her that she would be permitted a ride in the surrounding fields.

Clare, who was with them, said, "Father, may I go?"

He hesitated, then said, "I suppose," speaking almost as sourly to his own daughter as he spoke to any of them. In a gesture of rare kindness, Paulet brought the best horses he could find. He personally rode beside the queen and both seemed in such high spirits that, to Mary Seton's astonishment, once they actually smiled at each other. This alone should have made Mary Seton suspicious, but all she thought was how nice it was to have a few moments respite from the endless bickering and exchange of insults.

They returned to the castle to find a troop of more than a hundred horsemen waiting for them. For one delicious moment, before she saw that they were wearing the crest of the duke of Suffolk, Mary Seton thought they had come to rescue the queen.

Paulet said, "Clare, return to your room."

When Clare stared at him without moving, he shouted: "Go!" She dismounted and ran off, but not before Mary Seton saw her genuine fright.

One man, wearing partial armor and the Suffolk crest, dismounted and walked toward the queen. "Madam, we are here by orders of the royal government. We have been sent to arrest your two secretaries, Claude Nau and Gilbert Curl. A plot to assassinate the queen of England has been uncovered and your two secretaries are suspected of knowing the details."

Two horsemen wearing pistols at their belts and carrying chains approached Gilbert Curl, and one of them ordered him to dismount.

"They shall not," the queen said. "My servants shall not be put in chains like common criminals."

Paulet turned to the man wearing partial armor. "Has evidence been found to confirm our suspicions?"

"Yes, sir."

"Then her secretaries shall be taken to London."

A dozen horsemen then surrounded the queen. One rider took her reins. "And where, pray tell, are you taking me?"

"The manor of Tixall has been prepared for you," Paulet said.

"I shall go as well, of course," said Mary Seton.

"You will stay here," said Paulet. "The queen is going alone."

"Alone!" Jane Kennedy said. "Who shall attend her?"

Nobody answered Jane. Mary Seton and the others watched, disbelieving, as the queen was led away.

Back in their apartments, Mary Seton and Jane Kennedy found everything in disarray. Cupboards had been searched, her locks broken, all of her possessions taken. Paulet came in later to tell them that Nau and Gilbert Curl had been taken through the streets of London as bells pealed and people shouted with joy that Queen Elizabeth had been saved by their insidious plots.

Five days later, Mary Stuart returned. She was perfectly composed, her face set in an expression of calm defiance. "I saw Cecil at Tixall," she said. "He said I'm being charged with treason against the queen of England and he asked for a full confession. The queen of England herself wrote to me, telling me that a full confession was the only way to avoid open trial."

"Trial?" said Jane Kennedy. "She wouldn't dare!"

"Let her put me on trial. She knows the peers of England have no right to try me. How can I be charged with treason when I am queen of an independent realm? Let her take my life. So much the worse for her, if she does! The only possible victory I have left is to show the world how unjustly I have been treated all these years."

"But not a trial!" Jane said.

The queen smiled. "I learned that it was all a trick, every bit of it. Clifford Gifford hadn't been sent by my uncle, he was planted by Walsingham. Everything I wrote which is being held against me, I was tricked into writing. Walsingham, you can believe, is pleased with his work."

Later Jane Kennedy took Mary Seton aside: "She mustn't consent to a trial. Please try to talk her out of it. Only you can talk her out of it. They'll murder her!"

Mary Seton remembered the day in Edinburgh when she had signed her abdication because she saw hope of escape. She had sworn that the last words she uttered on earth would be the words of a queen of Scotland. Then she had been twenty three and alive with energy. Now she was ill, her son grown to manhood, and all hope of restoration was faded.

"She believes she will regain her dignity if allowed to speak for herself in public," Mary Seton said. "Maybe she's right."

The queen had never been afraid of death. It was with some pride that Mary Seton realized how her queen had matured from the sweet, naive, and trusting young woman she had once been. Like an ancient heroine achieving redemption through heroic suffering, Mary Queen of Scots was ready to face the English gentry and show a new face to the world.

"How can you talk this way?" Jane Kennedy demanded. "You, who have been with her longer than anyone else. Can you stand by quietly while they execute her?"

"Her greatest fear," Mary said, "is to die in obscurity, forgotten in English prisons. She wants to speak, and have the world listen."

But Jane didn't give up pleading with the queen to avoid a trial. "Elizabeth will pardon you, she will never-"

"I want none of her pardons," said the queen. "If I confess, she will triumph over me and I will be broken and humbled before the world. I plan to stand up and proclaim the injustices which the queen of England has committed, and I will die for my church. There is nothing more I can do in this world."

On the morning of her trial, the great hall was filled with people: Earls and barons journeyed from all over England to witness the trial and to see, for the first time, England's famous captive. Because the queen was not permitted to have her ladies accompany her – the judges were afraid they would make a scene – Mary Seton waited with the others to hear the outcome. Jane Kennedy and the others wept, terrified for the queen, but Mary Seton prayed that she was, indeed, having her final victory, that at last her words were being recorded for the tribunal of history.

Mary Seton had no doubt what the outcome would be: The queen of Scots would be convicted of high treason and condemned to death. With Philip preparing to launch the Armada against England, the Protestants would not take a chance on the successful rescue of the Scottish queen. However, none of it seemed real yet. Try as she might, she couldn't imagine the world without Mary Stuart.

# Destiny

The sun was setting and the queen's servants were lighting the night candles when the queen at last returned to her apartments. Too ill for supper, she said she would go to bed immediately. Before closing her door behind her, she kissed Mary Seton's cheek and said, "It all went as I hoped. My words moved even the harshest of my judges. They heard me at last. Pray now that the end comes as I want it."

# POSTLUDE
# FOTHERINGAY CASTLE,

The queen of Scots was kneeling at her prayers when the knock came at the door. She glanced up, but then continued her prayers, ignoring the second and third knocks as well. When she finished, Jane Kennedy helped her stand up. She gestured for Willie to open the door.

The sheriff of Northampton stood on the doorway. "Madam, the lords have sent me to you."

"I'm ready," she said.

Mary Seton and Jane Kennedy walked behind the queen as the sheriff led her down the long corridor to the staircase. Two guards opened the doors and stood aside to let them enter. When she stepped inside, the whispering and murmuring of the assembled crowds quieted.

In the center of the hall was a wooden stage lifted three steps off the floor, and on the stage was the block, draped in black. In front of the block was a cushion on which the queen was to kneel. Mary Seton recognized the cushion: it was one of the queen's finest, made of Italian velvet. Three earls sat in special chairs on the stage, and beside them, stood the executioner and his assistant, both dressed in black.

As the queen approached the stage, the Earl of Kent read aloud the commission for her execution. When he stopped speaking, the queen turned to face the members of the English gentry who, had things turned out differently, might have gathered to proclaim her queen of England. "With all my heart," she said, "I forgive my enemies, who have long sought my blood."

Jane Kennedy was crying, and Mary Seton wanted to cry, too. Later in private she would cry, mourning for Mary Stuart as she had mourned for Alexander. But for now she wanted to show the public as brave a face as the queen, who was just then climbing the three steps as if she were mounting the steps of a throne. It was Jane who kissed the queen's kerchief and tied it over her face, creating a turban over her eyes and the top of her head.

The executioner said, "Forgive me, Madam, for the deed I am about to commit."

"I forgive you with all my heart," she said, "for you shall at last make an end to Mary Stuart's troubles."

With the queen's eyes bound, she held the arm of the executioner's assistant and knelt on the cushion. She felt for the block, and finding it, laid down her head. Mary Seton watched as the executioner lifted the axe, but she squeezed her eyes closed and fought against the sickness in her stomach as she listened to the dull sound of steel cutting through flesh.

During the weeks that followed, Mary Seton's only companion was Clare. After the execution, which Clare had not been permitted to watch, a change came over the girl. She no longer begged for stories about the queen's glamorous, checkered, and tragic life. She seemed somber, even sad, as if the queen of Scots' death had touched her personally.

It was Clare who told Mary Seton that when Queen Elizabeth was told about the execution, she had a fit of anger declaring that she had never intended the execution to be carried out. She even imprisoned those of her servants who had delivered the warrant.

"Why does she do it?" Clare asked.

"Because she doesn't want to take the blame, because above all else she is concerned with her public image. I'm sure, too, she's vexed by what she's done, what she felt she had to do."

"But nobody believes her."

"Maybe she thinks eventually people will."

The winter was stormy and icy, but Mary Seton was numbed to the cold. She waited patiently as the months of winter crept by, knowing that she would soon be freed.

Early in spring, Clare and her family left the castle and returned to London. Mary Seton kissed her goodbye and gave her permission to write to her at the convent. When Clare threw her arms around Mary Seton's neck and said she'd miss her terribly, Mary Seton turned the girl's face up and kissed her cheek.

"The emptier this castle becomes," she said, "the more it feels like a prison."

In May, queen Elizabeth gave Mary Seton permission to journey to France. Her nephew, George's eldest son, applied for permission for her to travel on an English flagship to guarantee her safety across the Channel. He journeyed to England to escort her to France. On the way, they spent a night on one of the Norton's manors, a glorious house which she might have presided over as Lady Norton.

The journey to France took a week. She and her nephew, with a small riding party, crossed the French countryside to Rheims. Each time they entered a town and the townspeople learned that a maid of honor to the queen of Scots was passing through, they came forward and asked for the honor of kissing her hand.

Mary Seton accepted their sympathy, answering all their questions about the Scottish queen's trial and execution. Most were too young to remember the time when Mary Stuart sat on the French throne, but they still referred to her as their former queen. Mary Seton repeated many of the speeches the queen had prepared for her trial, knowing that Mary Stuart would be happy that the story of how bravely she died was being spread all over France.

At long last they approached the iron gates of the convent of St. Pierre. The lush lawns spread out as far as she could see, the flowers of May opened to the bright sunshine. All though the years of hell and chaos in Scotland and all through the years she had lived as a prisoner in England, each spring these gardens had come to life, just as she remembered. She wandered down the path overgrown with vegetation that led from the convent's gates to the river, feeling again the excitement she had known as a young girl hiding here, breathing the sweet smell of the damp earth mixed with the fragrant lilies in her own, secret haven.

# AFTERWARD

One year after the execution of Mary Queen of Scots, King Philip of Spain launched the Armada against England. When the English navy defeated the Spanish, England emerged for the first time as a major European power. The last years of Elizabeth's reign were years of cultural as well as military greatness. These were the years of Shakespeare, Raleigh, Spenser, and others. England's triumph was Elizabeth Tudor's triumph and she gave her name to the age.

Elizabeth died in 1602 at the age of 70 and was succeeded by Mary Stuart's son, King James of Scotland, and for the first time the crowns of England and Scotland were united. One of James's first acts as king of England was to move his mother's body to its final resting place, Kingston Abbey, the burial vault of the kings and queens of England. Mary Stuart's descendants include all the kings and queens of Great Britain, down to the present day.

Mary Seton lived the remainder of her life at the Convent of St. Pierre at Rheims. She lived to see Elizabeth's triumph and she lived to see Mary Stuart's son wear the English crown. There is no exact record of Mary Seton's death, but a copy of her last will and testament is dated 1609, when she was 72 years old. In her will, she requested that the jewels and gifts she received from the queen of Scots be kept in the Seton family, and she left provisions for the High Mass to be said for the soul of Mary Stuart..

# ABOUT ANNE KINSEY

To learn more about Anne and her forthcoming fiction, please visit Anne's website at http://www.AnneKinsey.com. If you have any comments or questions, she would love to hear from you.

www.ingramcontent.com/pod-product-compliance
Lightning Source LLC
Chambersburg PA
CBHW020947180626
46814CB00003B/965